"Locked In?"

Jacinda gasped, staring at Anthony in dismay as the meaning of his words sank in. They spent the next several minutes flinging their combined weight against the thick wood in an effort to break the lock.

"It's no use, Jacinda," he said at last. "We have been compromised, and we have no other course open to us except marriage."

"Marriage!" she exclaimed.

"Of course, marriage!" he replied. "My word, Jacinda, what kind of man do you take me for? It's my fault your reputation has been ruined. Naturally I shall do the honorable thing."

"Well, thank you very much, Your Grace! The proposal every girl dreams of, I am sure!"

Anthony uttered a strangled oath at her willfulness. "If this isn't the proposal you have longed for, Miss Malvern, then neither is it the way I imagined myself making an offer. But there is nothing else to be done. We're getting married, Jacinda, and that's the end of it."

"How very noble of you, Your Grace, but before you fling yourself on the sacrificial altar, might I suggest we try one other thing?"

"What?" He scowled at her sharp words.

"Ring for the valet and have him bring the key."

~~~❦~~~

The Journals of Lady X

Also by
Joan Overfield

THE PRODIGAL SPINSTER

Published by
PAGEANT BOOKS

The Journals of Lady X

Joan Overfield

PAGEANT BOOKS

PAGEANT BOOKS
225 Park Avenue South
New York, New York 10003

Cover artwork by Elaine Gignilliat

Printed in the U.S.A.

First Pageant Books printing: April, 1989

10 9 8 7 6 5 4 3 2 1

In memory of June Cavanaugh, who always told me to keep writing, no matter what

Prologue

London, 1811

"You're late."

Anthony Selton, Duke of Marchfield, turned at the clipped words, his hand closing around the small pistol he carried in his pocket. When he saw the blond man sitting in the chair with his back to the fireplace, he relaxed visibly. "My apologies, Sir," he said, unbuttoning his many-caped greatcoat and draping it across the worn green-and-white-striped chair. "But I was gaming at a friend's club, and I fear it took the boy some time to find me. I came as quickly as I could."

"Your friend's name?" Blue eyes studied Anthony coolly as he restored his hair to order before settling in the chair.

"Holbrecht." Anthony was unperturbed by his host's terse manner. As one of Sir's operatives for the past three years, he was accustomed to his superior's sometimes abrupt manners.

1

A cold smile touched Sir's lips. "And did you lose?"

Anthony's ice-colored eyes sparkled in momentary derision. "Just enough to keep him happy," he replied, leaning his velvet-clad shoulders against the sagging cushions of the ancient chair. Like the rest of the furnishings in the small room, the chair had seen better days, but it fit the image Sir deliberately cultivated: that of an unrepentant rake who lived on his wits. Having just come from the club, Anthony was still in evening dress, and his cream-colored silk pantaloons and immaculate black velvet jacket contrasted sharply with the genteel shabbiness of the rented rooms.

"He invited me up to his estate for a week-long shoot," Anthony continued, crossing one elegantly shod foot over the other. "If he and the others were involved in the selling of those supplies to the French, I'll soon have them. Is that why you wished to see me?"

In answer Sir tossed him the book he had been holding on his lap. "Have you read this?"

Anthony turned over the slender volume, a black eyebrow raising in surprise at the gold letters stamped into the deep red leather. *"The Journals of Lady X,"* he read aloud, his tone faintly mocking. " 'Being the fictional adventures of a Lady of Fashion's visit to Foreign Courts.' Good gad, Sir, 'tis nothing but drivel! Malicious tattlemongering of the worst sort!"

"I didn't ask you for a literary critique, Marchfield." Sir's voice was dangerously soft. "I asked if you had read it."

"Yes, Sir!" Anthony straightened at once, his

years of training evident in his response. " 'Tis considered fashionable for everyone in Society to have read the wretched thing."

"And your professional opinion?"

Anthony frowned in confusion, wondering why a book such as this should have attracted the attention of England's top spy master. As the leader of a secret group of highly trained men operating in England against the agents of Napoleon, it was Sir's job to ferret out any evidence of espionage. That he had been able to do so virtually undetected for over five years was mute testimony to his skills. If he was interested in the *Journals,* then something was definitely amiss.

"It is as I have said," Anthony began, carefully recalling all that he had read. "The book 'tis naught but a clever piece of libel masquerading as a work of fiction. Many of the more prominent members of the ton are easily recognizable, as are several incidents from the past three seasons." He paused, a reluctant smile softening his firm mouth. "The author has a wickedly cutting sense of humor, and I must own I rather enjoyed her skillful play on words. But I can't say that I noticed anything which might have been of interest to you. Unless it was the way certain . . . er . . . persons were portrayed?" He glanced questioningly at his superior.

"Actually," Sir said, his sea-blue eyes taking on an amused glow, "the Regent was delighted at the way this Lady X depicted him. Like you, he appreciates her wry wit. But that isn't why I mentioned the matter. Did you notice anything else?"

"She did devote several passages to various battles and the like which closely resembles our own campaigns to regain the peninsula," Anthony volunteered, rubbing his chin thoughtfully. "But I can't recall any specific de—"

"Open the book to the page I have marked and read the circled passage," Sir instructed, placing his feet on the faded hassock. "Aloud, if you please."

Anthony did as ordered, flipping the book open to the page marked with a slender gold ribbon. " *'Twas a wonderment to all that with so many prettily dressed soldiers littering up the ballrooms and assemblies, Lady Thistlebottom had yet to secure a lover. One would think, gentle reader, that with over five thousand troops stationed in the capital city and another two thousand quartered nearby, she would have found someone to suit her needs. She was not, after all, widely known for either her discretion or her good taste.'* " He broke off with a chuckle, remembering Lady Jersey's outrage at the speculation that she was the real Lady Thistlebottom, then his eyes widened in horror.

"Good lord, we have five thousand troops quartered in London!" he said, staring at Sir in shock. "How the devil could she have known that?"

"Those are my sentiments," Sir responded, rising to his feet to stand before the meager fire flickering in the grate. "Odd, is it not, that she was able to name the *exact* number of men? A number, I might add, that is known but to a few?"

"Perhaps it was sheer chance," Anthony ven-

tured, silently cursing himself for his inattentive-
ness.

"Perhaps. Turn to page one forty-five."

Again, Anthony did as he was bid, thumbing
through the book until he reached the circled
paragraph. " *'Another remarkable thing about the court is
that several persons who enjoy the Pineapple King's Patron-
age are said to possess the ability to render themselves invisi-
ble, thus enabling them to move about the company of their
fellows unobserved, gathering information which they then
relate to His Royal Highness.'* Christ!" The book fell
from his hands as he raised his stunned gray eyes
and met Sir's implacable gaze.

"You may see my concern," Sir said quietly, his
dark gold eyebrows meeting over his aquiline
nose. "In all the years the Prince of Wales has
supported us there has never been any link between our activities and Carlton House—until
now."

"Then you think this Lady X is an enemy
agent?" Anthony asked, staring down at the book
with revulsion.

"I'm sure of it." Sir shoved his hands into the
pockets of his tattered green and gold dressing
gown. "And a highly placed spy at that. Much of
the information which has been passed along can
only be described as sensitive at best. The majority of it is unknown outside the Home Office,
which is why it was able to slip past the censors.
And as you say, 'tis not but a piece of fiction.
Why should it be suspect?"

"*You* suspected it," Anthony said bitterly, tossing the book onto the table. "Whoever this Lady
X is, he's good. He's damned good."

"I agree, Marchfield," Sir said, pulling a sealed letter from his pocket and handing it to Anthony. "Your orders. Since much of the gossip deals with the ton, I think that should be the best place to start our search. I want you to discover Lady X's identity."

"And then?"

Sir's eyes hardened with chilling anger. "And then I want you to silence him. Permanently."

Chapter One

"Jacinda! What the deuce is keeping you, gel? Jacinda! Come out of there at once!"

"Coming, Uncle Hugh!" Jacinda Malvern hastily closed her notebook at the sound of her uncle's voice outside the library door. "I shan't be but another moment, sir!"

"Well, make it quick, can't you." She heard him mumble disagreeably as he turned away, "Haven't got all day, you know." She waited until she heard his footsteps moving down the stairs before collapsing against the back of her chair.

"That was a close one, Purrfect," she sighed, addressing the large white Persian cat who was stretched indolently across the top of the shiny cherry-wood desk. "Another moment and the old rasher of wind would have found us out!"

Purrfect closed one amber-colored eye, clearly unconcerned with the danger that had just passed. "Well, 'tis easy for you to be so calm," Jacinda continued, her hazel eyes sparkling with laughter as she rose to her feet. "I'm the one who would have been disgraced forever if they should discover what I've *really* been doing up here." She shook out the skirts of her gray merino gown before crossing the oak-paneled room to the wall of towering bookshelves. After a moment's consideration she tucked the precious notebook between two heavy volumes sporting Greek lettering on their spines.

"There," she said, a smile of pure mischief lighting her quiet features as she stepped back to admire her handiwork. "I've hidden it between *The Complete Works of Plato* and *The Odyssey.* That should keep it safe from Uncle's hands."

After putting away her quills and paper, she paused long enough to tuck a strand of light brown hair back into her chignon before hurrying down the stairs to find her uncle. The butler was standing beside the parlor door, and at her approach his wooden features softened into something resembling a smile.

"Her ladyship and your cousin have just joined his lordship," he informed her in his grave manner. "I believe this may have something to do with last night's . . . er . . . unfortunate accident."

Jacinda made a face, her small nose wrinkling in distaste. "I thought as much," she said with a resigned sigh. "Ah, well. There's nothing for it, I suppose, but to pay the piper. Thank you for the warning, Wilkens."

"You're most welcome, Miss Jacinda." He

bowed stiffly. "I shall wait fifteen minutes before bringing in the tea. If that is acceptable?"

"Quite acceptable," Jacinda agreed, secretly admiring the butler's devious turn of mind. Her aunt and uncle were both passionately fond of their food, and if anything could distract them from ringing a peal over her head, it would be a pot of hot tea and a plate of Cook's freshly baked cakes. She flashed the butler a conspiratorial smile, then schooled her face to show no expression before entering the parlor.

"Well, 'tis about time you saw fit to join us." Her uncle, Hugh Creighton, the Earl of Shipton, grumbled as she entered the scarlet-and-cream-colored parlor. "Did I not send for you well over an hour ago?"

Actually, it had been less than fifteen minutes, but with so much at stake, Jacinda decided not to debate the issue. "Yes, Uncle," she said, making her voice as meek as possible as she slid onto the rose-and-cream-colored settee. "But I was busy copying down one of Lord Perceval's speeches, and you do know how he hates to be interrupted."

"Er . . . yes . . . quite." Her uncle clearly did not know how to reply. As a good Tory, he had no wish to offend his party's leader. Clearing his throat, he lumbered to his feet, placing his beefy hands on the lapels of his somber black velvet jacket. "Now, Jacinda," he began, sounding for all the world as if he were about to address Parliament, "I'm sure you're aware that your actions of last evening cannot pass unremarked. Spilling a cup of punch on Lord

Treadway's new jacket is the outside of enough, even for you. What have you to say for yourself?"

"I'm sorry, Uncle Hugh." Jacinda hung her head, more to hide the resentful gleam in her eyes than out of any feeling of maidenly shame. Lord Treadway was a bothersome old lecher who had pawed her all evening. It had taken her the better part of an hour to maneuver into a position where she could "accidentally" fling the contents of her punch cup on him. But the expression of horror on his florid face as he watched the crimson-colored stain spreading inexorably across the front of his oyster satin jacket had been well worth her pains. "I did offer to replace his lordship's coat," she added in what she hoped was an anxious manner. "But he seemed to take the greatest exception to my suggestion."

"Well, of course he did, you ninnyhammer!" Her Aunt Prudence, Lady Shipton, exclaimed, eyeing her niece with marked impatience. "He is a marquess, after all, and no man who fancies himself a gentleman would ever allow a lady to replace an article of clothing! By making such an offer, you were implying his lordship is *not* all that he should be."

Jacinda was careful to hide her smile. Good, she thought smugly. It was nice to know that her subtle insult hadn't gone unnoticed, although it did mean that at least some of the ton was more clever than she had first credited. She'd have to mind her step lest they prove to be *too* clever.

"I assure you I meant no such thing, ma'am," she said, raising her hazel eyes to her aunt's face.

"Indeed, it would never have occurred to me to imply such a thing of so worthy a gentleman! I merely thought that as it was my clumsiness that caused the accident, then it was only logical that I be the one to replace his coat."

"I realize that," her uncle replied, resuming his seat. "But such things are simply not done. I know that you are from the country, but after all these years I should have thought you would have acquired some town bronze! 'Tis bad enough that you have set yourself up as a blue-stocking, but this, this is really too much! I must caution you yet again to mind your behavior, Jacinda. It is common knowledge that we have taken you in as one of our family, and your every action therefore is a reflection upon us. Have I your word that you will henceforth behave in a manner more befitting a female in your position?"

"Yes, Uncle Hugh." Jacinda held on to her temper with a will. One of the family, indeed, she seethed. And the "position" her uncle alluded to was doubtlessly that of a poor relation dependent upon her family's good graces for her daily bread. Or at least that is how they had treated her since they had first insisted she make her home with them following the death of her own parents four years ago. Then as now, she endured their hospitality only because she had no choice. But she was no longer seventeen and someday, she promised herself resentfully, someday she would show them all!

"Well, it's all a perfect hum, if you ask me!" Her cousin, Lady Cassandra, who heretofore had remained blessedly silent, gave a tinkling laugh, her dark eyes sliding over Jacinda's plainly clad figure. "After all, it's not really as if you were a person of any importance, cousin!"

Jacinda's cheeks burned at Cassandra's well-aimed barb. Her cousin had been disagreeable enough while still in the schoolroom, but now that she was a debutante she had grown quite unendurable. Fortunately, she was as rich and lovely as she was mean and spiteful, and Jacinda didn't doubt but that some poor, misguided man would be making her an offer before the season was ended.

"That's quite enough, Cassandra," Lady Shipton reproved her daughter with a gentle scold. "How many times must I tell you a lady never reminds others of their misfortune? I'm sure your cousin is aware that her birth in no way approaches your own. And as for you, young lady"—she next turned her malevolent gaze upon Jacinda—"mind what your uncle has told you. The next time you spill punch on a gentleman's jacket you are to come directly to us. Do you understand?"

Jacinda ignored her aunt's insult, wondering if the older woman was aware she had just granted her carte blanche to ruin the coat of every obnoxious man in London. Considering the number of wretched creatures, it was a task that could keep her happily occupied for months! "Yes, Auntie Prudence," she demurred, her eyes beginning to sparkle in eager anticipation. "I promise the very next time I spill anything I shall inform you or Uncle Hugh at once."

"See that you do," her aunt said briskly, turning toward the door as the footman appeared with the tea cart. "Oh, good," she exclaimed, her eyes taking on an eager glow at the sight of the fruit tarts, cucumber sandwiches, and other delicacies that had been lavishly piled high. "Ah, here's the tea. Cassandra, dearest, why don't you pour?"

Almack's of a Wednesday night was filled to overflowing with the crème de la crème of society, all jostling and pushing each other as they made their way up the grand staircase. From his post beside the Countess Dechiens, Anthony surveyed the glittering throng coldly, his light gray eyes coming to rest on the plump, balding man in the scarlet jacket and yellow waistcoat who had just made his bows to the patronesses. It was Hugh Creighton, the Earl of Shipton, and unless Anthony was much mistaken, the infamous Lady X.

"*Tiens,* Your Grace," the countess said with a merry giggle, playfully swatting his arm with her fan. "Such a dark look as you are shooting at Shipton! Could it be that you are a suitor for the fair Cassandra and he has rejected your offer? Surely the man is not *that* big a gudgeon!"

"Not at all, my lady." Anthony swiftly schooled his features to reflect his customary indifference. "If I appear to be observing the earl with aversion, it is because I take great exception to his lordship's coat. Whatever could his man have been thinking to let him go about dressed so?" And he lifted his quizzing glass to his eye, his sneer deepening as he took in the badly cut jacket with its oversize brass buttons and unfashionably large lapels.

The countess gave a delighted laugh. "He does look the perfect cake, *non?*" she agreed, hiding her smirk behind her fan. "And that disagreeable wife of his is little better. Ruffles and white tulle at her age; can you imagine? Ah, well, at least the daughter is a diamond of the first water," she drawled, her dark blue eyes sliding to Cassandra, who was trailing after her papa, her well-proportioned figure swathed in glittering white silk. "All that lovely dark hair, and those magnificent brown eyes! And there is her fortune to consider, of course. Are you quite sure you aren't harboring the slightest tendre for her?"

"Ah, that would be telling, your ladyship," Anthony prevaricated with the skill of long practice. "Although I must admit I have found myself giving the lovely young lady more and more thought these past few weeks."

"Ah, you *anglais.*" The countess shook her head mournfully. "How backwards you are when it comes to affairs of the heart! Thinking about a young lady will never win her; first you must court her!"

"First you must *meet* her," Anthony corrected, hiding a pleased smile at how smoothly everything was progressing. He had decided to use the daughter to trap the father, but because he didn't move in the same circles as the earl, he was uncertain how to strike up an acquaintance with the beauteous Lady Cassandra. Now, apparently, fate had decided to lend him a hand. He gave the countess his most accomplished smile. "We haven't been introduced as yet," he added, lest she fail to take the hint.

"Then that is something I must remedy at once!" she answered decisively, obviously pleased with the notion of playing cupid. "Come." She fastened her hand on the duke's arm and began dragging him toward Cassandra and her family. "I shall introduce you *toute de suite.*"

Jacinda saw the duke approaching before Cassandra did. She had spied the handsome but aloof Marchfield when they had first entered the Assembly Room, and she wondered why he had decided to grace Almack's with his exalted presence. Everyone knew he was so insufferably high in the instep as to consider even that holiest of the holies beneath his touch. But before she had time to speculate on the matter, the duke and the Countess Dechiens were upon them.

"Ah, good evening to you, my lord, my lady," the countess said, dropping a graceful curtsy that belied her advanced years. "So wonderful to see you and your charming daughter again."

"My lady." The earl bowed as much as his stays would allow, his dark eyes resting with marked suspicion upon Anthony, who was standing patiently beside the countess. "And you, sir, I can't say as I have had the pleasure, although your face is somewhat familiar."

"My lord, I should like to introduce you to Anthony Selton, Duke of Marchfield." Countess Dechiens performed the introduction with the Gallic love of drama, her eyes bright with laughter as she shot Anthony a mischievous wink. "The duke was just commenting on your jacket, my lord."

Lord Shipton brightened at that. "Were you?" He gave Anthony a benevolent smile, deciding to overlook the fact that the duke was descended from a long line of loose-living Torys on his mother's side. "My tailor is an excellent man, excellent. I should be happy to give you his direction, Your Grace."

"You are too kind," Anthony replied, turning to smile at Lady Shipton and Lady Cassandra.

"Allow me to make you known to m'family." The earl was quick to assume his parental duties. "This is m'wife, Countess of Shipton, and m'daughter, Lady Cassandra Creighton. Daresay you already know m'son, Lord Wilmount Creighton."

"Indeed I do," Anthony replied, recalling a petulant young dandy scarce into his twenties. "I do not see him with you; I trust he is well?"

"Oh, yes, quite," the earl assured him, his plump chest swelling with pride as he spoke of his son and heir. "Decided to sit part of the season out, don't you know. He's devoted to the land, is my Wilmount."

"I see." Anthony already knew of Wilmount's location, of course. He had left nothing to chance in his investigation of Shipton. His gray eyes rested on the final member of the Shipton party, and he stared at her pointedly until the earl caught the hint.

"This other's m'niece, Miss Jacinda Malvern," he said, indicating Jacinda with a casual wave of his hand. "Jacinda, make your curtsies to his grace."

"Your Grace." Jacinda did as ordered, delighted at the opportunity to observe the duke at closer quarters. She had seen him several times, of course, but she had yet to make his acquaintance. She hoped he would be as proud and haughty as he was reputed to be.

"Miss Malvern." Anthony acknowledged her with a polite inclination of his head, taking dispassionate note of her plain gown of gray and blue silk. He knew her to be the family's poor relation who had resided with the Creightons for the past four years, and he made a mental note to question her when the opportunity presented itself. It had always been his experience that servants and poor relations were often an invaluable source of information.

A strain of music caught his ear, and he turned to Cassandra with a practiced smile. "Lady Cassandra"—the most exacting dance master could not have faulted the elegant bow he bestowed upon her—"dare I hope you have not promised this dance to another? I am convinced you must be as graceful as you are lovely, and I would deem it a great honor to lead you out. With your father's permission, of course."

"Of course, of course," Lord Shipton assured him, his ruddy face glowing with paternal pride. "Be more than happy for you to escort m'daughter, but unfortunately she has already promised this dance to Lord Grantville. Perhaps another time, eh, Marchfield?"

"Of course." Anthony was too well trained to

allow his frustration to show. He stood and chatted with the Creightons until Lady Cassandra's partner, a gray-haired marquess with notoriously deep pockets, came to claim her. Despite this setback he still had hopes of ingratiating himself with the earl, but unfortunately the earl and his lady had other obligations, and after dropping several hints that his company at tea would not be unwelcomed, they took their leave. The countess had long since drifted away, leaving him alone with Jacinda.

"Have you been in London long, Miss Malvern?" he asked politely, deciding he might as well question her now as later. "I am certain I have not seen your face before."

Considering the lengths she went to to remain unnoticed when out in society, Jacinda didn't doubt this for one minute. Still, she couldn't help but feel the smallest sense of pique that the duke should think her newly arrived from the country. "I have been here four years, Your Grace," she said, her pointed chin coming up as she met his gaze.

"Have you?" Anthony sensed the challenge in her words, and puzzled at the reason. He knew she had the reputation of a bluestocking, and he wondered if she was one of those learned females who considered men as bothersome bores. Lord, he hoped not. He had better things to do with his time than to match wits with a sharp-tongued termagant. His gaze drifted to the dance floor, his eyes easily finding Lady Cassandra and her portly swain among the other couples.

Jacinda noted the direction of his stare, and her

resentment was instantly forgotten. It would be beyond all that was wonderful if her shrewish cousin had managed to fix Marchfield's interest, she thought with a flash of malicious amusement. Not that she wished the duke ill, precisely, but she did think the two rather deserved each other.

Aware of Miss Malvern's continued silence, Anthony made one final stab at polite conversation. "And how do you spend your days in London, Miss Malvern?" he asked, giving her a patently insincere smile. "At the bookstores and lending libraries, I shouldn't doubt." As an avid reader, he was hoping to find some topic of common interest with her.

"Oh, yes, I am quite the quiz," Jacinda answered sweetly, deciding that the duke was proving to be a most intriguing subject for Lady X. Not only was he wonderfully condescending, but he was also devilishly attractive. Most of the men in Lady X's journals were plumpish, preening dandies, and she rather thought her readers would welcome a handsome and wealthy character. Yes, he would do quite nicely.

Anthony caught the amused sparkle in Miss Malvern's hazel eyes and drew himself up stiffly. He had done everything in his power to be polite to the chit, and now she was laughing at him. Very well, he decided, regarding her down the length of his patrician nose, if she wished to be so rude, then he saw no reason why he should remain with her. Besides, the waltz had ended, and if he hurried he might be able to get Lady Cassandra to himself for a few minutes of flirting. It was obvious he would learn nothing crossing verbal swords with Miss Malvern.

"If you will excuse me, ma'am, I believe I see an old friend," he said, his eyebrows rising as he turned to face her. "You will pardon me, I am sure."

"Oh, of course, Your Grace," Jacinda murmured, making a mental note of the eyebrows. It was just the sort of gesture she could give her character in her next book.

Anthony gave her a sharp look, not caring for her tone of voice. He had the feeling she was laughing up her sleeve at him, and the idea did not please him. In the next moment he was impatiently brushing the thought aside, telling himself he had more important matters to attend to. After dropping a brief bow, he departed, his back stiff with anger as he walked away.

Jacinda watched him go, her lips lifting in a wicked smile as she studied his rigid posture. Stiff back, she thought, a scheme forming slowly in her mind. Stiff back. Yes, the very thing! In the next journal Lady X would have a new target to skewer with her pen. Lord Stiffback, the most arrogant man ever to grace a court!

Chapter Two

Jacinda was up early the following morning, her fingers fairly itching to resume work on the latest installment of the *Journals*. As she intended to spend the morning in the library she dressed to suit herself in a comfortable gown of pale blue muslin, with a fichu of ivory-colored lace draped across her shoulders to protect them from the ever-present draft that pervaded the room. She was trying to decide whether to don one of the caps she had recently purchased or to pin her hair back in a chignon, when there was a knock at her door.

"Excuse me, Miss Jacinda." A harried-looking maid entered dropping a polite curtsy. "But there be a gentleman in the parlor asking to see her ladyship."

"So early?" Jacinda's hazel eyes went to the dainty clock on her dressing table to confirm the hour. "Why, it's not even eleven o'clock!"

"I know, miss," the maid replied with a troubled sigh. "Her ladyship is up, but she's not dressed as yet, and she asks please if you will entertain the gentleman until she and Lady Cassandra can join you."

"Of course," Jacinda said, hiding her disappointment from the maid. She had little use for the social scene—except when she could sit unobserved in a corner chair, scribbling down its foibles—and she shuddered to think of the tiresome young buck she would be forced to entertain in her aunt's stead. One of Cassie's ardent suitors, no doubt. "Pray tell the gentleman I shall be with him shortly. Millie?" she called out just as the maid was leaving.

"Yes, Miss Jacinda?"

"What is the name of our caller?"

"Oh, a duke, miss!" the maid exclaimed, her blue eyes wide with awe. "The Duke of Marchfield, and he brought our Lady Cassandra the biggest bunch of roses you ever did see!"

"Ah, did he?" Jacinda's mouth tilted in a wicked smile. "Well, in that case, I suppose I really mustn't keep his grace waiting." And rising to her feet, she paused only long enough to brush her light brown hair back from her face before hurrying down to her aunt's front parlor.

Anthony waited in the sunlit room, his back to the fireplace as he glanced at his pocket watch every now and again. He had been waiting for over fifteen minutes, and his patience was almost at an end. His arrival was a trifle early by town standards, but it was hardly the middle of the night! He was about to ring for the footman to demand news of his hostess, when the door opened, and Miss Malvern stepped inside.

"Good morning, Your Grace," she said, favoring him with a polite smile. "What a pleasant surprise to find you here, and at so early an hour! I vow, we are honored by your eagerness."

A dull flush stained Anthony's cheeks, and he shot the pert Miss Malvern a resentful glare. Blast the creature, anyway, he brooded, inclining his head in acknowledgment to her greeting. With little more than a few words she had re-

duced him to the rank of an ill-mannered school-
boy, and his dislike of her increased proportion-
ately.

"Miss Malvern," he said, his voice as chilling
as the look he flashed her. "I apologize if my un-
timely arrival has inconvenienced you."

"Oh, not at all, Your Grace," Jacinda answered,
pleased that he was every bit as toplofty as he
appeared last night. "Dukes bearing roses are always welcome, regardless of the hour. But pray,
won't you be seated?" She indicated the crimson
velvet chair behind him with a casual wave of her
hand.

"Thank you," Anthony replied, taking his seat.
As he had several calls to make this morning, he
was dressed conservatively in a jacket of maroon-
colored superfine, his cravat tied in an intricate
arrangement beneath his chin. His breeches were
of buff nankin, and his Hessians had been shined
to a brilliant gloss. A single fob adorned his blue
waistcoat, and a gold signet ring flashed from a
tanned finger, adding a touch of elegance to his
austere appearance.

Jacinda noted all of this in a swift glance, tucking the information away for future use. She
liked to be as precise as possible when describing
her characters, and she was determined not to
slight Lord Stiffback in this respect—although it
might be intriguing to dandify him just a trifle.
An extra fob or two never hurt anyone, she decided, hiding a secretive smile.

Anthony caught her surreptitious perusal of
him, but wisely chose to ignore it. Although he
was by no means a vain man, he was not unaware

of the fact that the fairer sex found him attractive. And Miss Malvern, despite her sharp tongue and equally sharp mind, was, after all, a female. And although not dressed to advantage, she was a rather fetching one at that, he decided, his gray eyes resting on the light brown hair that cascaded down to her shoulders in shiny waves.

Jacinda felt his gaze on her and, realizing she was being somewhat derelict in her duties, flashed him an encouraging smile. "I was surprised to see you at Almack's last night, Your Grace," she said, figuring that, like most men, the duke was waiting to talk only of himself. "You don't usually attend such gatherings."

This observation surprised Anthony, for it had been months since he had last poked his head in the place. "My work with the government occupies much of my time," he told her with the natural wariness of the spy. "But I hadn't thought I had become quite so reclusive that it should cause talk."

"Oh, it hasn't," Jacinda returned cheerfully, a dimple flashing at the corner of her mouth. "I was merely making an observation. The curse of the bookish, I am afraid. We are an intolerably curious lot."

Her self-deprecating humor brought a reluctant smile to Anthony's face. "Yes, I have heard that is often the case," he said, giving her a warm look. "Have you read many articles on the subject?" He settled back against the soft cushions with every evidence of enjoying their somewhat unorthodox conversation.

"A few," she answered, torn between amusement and irritation. Really, it would be too vexing if his grace turned out to be *nice*. Lord Stiffback had been such a promising character!

The arrival of the footman bearing a light tea provided a welcome diversion. While Jacinda busied herself preparing the duke's plate she searched her mind for some topic that might provoke him. Calling upon the little she knew of him, she remembered he was a Tory, and she brightened with sudden inspiration.

"Actually," she began, handing him his cup and a plate of freshly baked macaroons, "the other day I did read a rather interesting article in one of the more . . . radical journals."

"Really, and what did the article concern?" he asked, raising his cup to his lips. "A literary treatise, perhaps?"

"Oh, no." She gave him her sweetest smile. "It was all about the Luddites. I quite support their actions, you know."

Anthony all but choked on his tea. "The Luddites!" he exclaimed, glowering at her in disapproval. "Whatever do you know of those machine wreckers?"

"Only what I have read," she admitted, delighted at the return of the duke's haughty demeanor. "I believe the poor men have no course other than the one they have chosen. When so many suffer from want and hunger and the government does nothing but add to their burdens, then what else can they do? Do you not agree?"

"I do not!" He set his cup down with an angry clatter. "You are speaking of anarchy, Miss Malvern! Rebellion! I find it difficult to believe that a lady of your breeding should support the smashing of machines, or that you would condone such wanton acts of violence! Does your uncle share these foolish notions?" he demanded suspiciously, wondering if, on top of everything else, the earl was an anarchist.

"Uncle?" Jacinda gave a tinkling laugh. "Heavens, no, sir! He is a Tory, like yourself, and what does a Tory care for the suffering of the lower classes?"

Such frankly partisan sentiments made Anthony stiffen in resentment. "A man need not be a Whig or a revolutionary to care for others, Miss Malvern," he said in a voice that was icy with suppressed fury. "I am not insensitive to the suffering of those about me; I am doing everything in my power to help them. But I draw the line at coddling rioters when we are at war. Or had that fact escaped your notice?"

"Oh, no," Jacinda assured him. "You'll find me wide awake on all accounts, Your Grace. And it is precisely because we are at war that I feel I must lend the Luddites my support."

"What do you mean?"

"Well." She paused, surprised to find that she was suddenly quite serious about what she was saying. "We say we are fighting to oppose Napoleon's dreadful tyranny; is that not so?" At his curt nod, she continued. "And yet, what can be more tyrannical than the great burden of poverty and hunger? Yes, what the Luddites are doing *is* wrong, I suppose, but so is it wrong to starve and beat our own people into submission. If we wish England to remain truly free of tyranny, then we must eliminate the great need that exists in our land. Otherwise, we are no better than the country we are fighting."

Her eloquence left Anthony speechless, and for a moment he could only gaze at her in reluctant admiration. Although he disapproved of her sentiments, he could not fault the sincerity with which she voiced them.

"Most eloquently phrased, Miss Malvern," he said quietly, his gaze resting on her flushed cheeks. "If your article should prove to be half so well expressed, I fear our streets will run as red with blood as they did in Paris."

"Ah, Your Grace, what a delightful surprise!" Lady Shipton exclaimed, sweeping into the parlor with Cassandra following close behind. "I trust we haven't kept you waiting overlong?"

"Not at all, my lady." Anthony rose to his feet to greet his hostess. He had been so involved in his discussion with Miss Malvern that he had quite forgotten the Creighton ladies. But now that he was reminded of his duty, he set out to charm his unsuspecting prey. "I only hope my eagerness has not inconvenienced either you or your lovely daughter." He turned a provocative smile on Cassandra, who beamed with delight.

"My heavens, no," Lady Shipton said with a laugh, gesturing Jacinda away from the tea cart. "Why, we are always up and about early like this, are we not, my love?"

"Oh, yes," Cassandra agreed with a flutter of her lashes. Today she wore a gown of red-and-cream-striped silk trimmed at the bodice with full sleeves with a fall of lace, and her dark hair was arranged in curls à la Juliet. Jacinda had to admit she looked most fetching, which only made her that much more aware of her own drab appearance.

"Thank you for keeping our guest company until we could arrive, Jacinda," Lady Shipton said, flashing her a falsely sweet smile. "I am sure you must be itching to get back to your reading. You may go now." She turned to the duke with another laugh. "Our little Jacinda is quite, quite blue, you know. I daresay I do not understand half of what she is saying!"

Such casual cruelty set Anthony's teeth on edge. Although he had no personal feelings for Miss Malvern, he did respect her, and he could not like the way her aunt dismissed her as if she were no more than a servant.

"Indeed?" His eyebrows arched over his gray eyes as he studied the countess's face. "How odd. I found Miss Malvern's conversation to be most illuminating. We were, in fact, discussing an article she recently read when you arrived."

"Were you? How interesting," Lady Shipton said in obvious disbelief. With a very beautiful and marriageable daughter on hand and a very eligible duke in her parlor it was obvious she did not intend wasting time discussing her tiresome niece. "Cassandra reads, as well. Oh, not prosy things such as my niece does, but poetry and the like. Her governess was most impressed with her intelligence; isn't that so, Jacinda?"

"Yes, Aunt Prudence," Jacinda responded dutifully.

"It runs in the family, studying does," the

countess prattled on. "My grandfather Bedford was quite a famous poet, now that I think of it. And in his salad days, my husband was forever scribbling away at something."

"Was he?" Anthony did his best to hide his interest at this unexpected bit of information. Perhaps he should report to Sir sooner than he had anticipated.

"Oh, my, yes." The countess poured some tea for her daughter and herself. "In fact, he still does, although he's very secretive about the whole thing. He never shows any of us what he writes. Just keeps it locked in his desk drawer most of the time. Ah, well." She shrugged her shoulders with wifely understanding. "Men must have their little secrets, I suppose. It makes them feel important."

All this talk of secretive writing left Jacinda feeling ill at ease. Her aunt had made it clear that she was definitely de trop, so perhaps it was time to stage a strategic retreat. Fortunately, her uncle chose that moment to arrive, and after staying long enough to listen to him boast of his newest piece of horseflesh, she rose to her feet.

"If you will excuse me, Aunt, Your Grace, I think perhaps I will return to my study. It was a pleasure seeing you again, sir," she added, holding her hand out to the duke. "I look forward to our next meeting."

"As do I." Anthony stood, accepting Miss Malvern's hand and carrying it to his lips for a brief kiss. "Perhaps by then I shall have a reply to the interesting question you posed. But then"—his gray eyes teased her with intimate laughter—"as a good Tory I am unable to resist a good debate."

His gentle raillery alarmed Jacinda almost as much as the touch of his lips on her hand, and it required all her self-control not to blush like a Bath miss. "Yes, the Tories are all very good at talk," she riposted with a quick smile. "Which is probably why the ladies find them so irresistible. Good day, sir."

After leaving the earl's mansion on Berkeley Square, Anthony went directly to Sir's lodgings in a crude hotel not far from Covent Garden. The slatternly proprietress showed a marked reluctance to admit him, but a shiny new shilling pressed into her dirt-stained palm did much to alter her attitude. She even promised to bring up a tea tray, and a second shilling won her agreement to give the cups an "extra special" washing.

He was surprised to find Sir still abed when he entered the bedroom, but when he was about to leave, Sir called out. "Never mind, Marchfield. 'Tis past time I was up," he said, covering a yawn with a huge fist. "Wait in the other room, and I shall be with you shortly. Oh, and ring for some tea, will you?" He ran a hand through his rumpled dark gold hair.

"Already done, Sir," Anthony answered, pulling the door closed. "I'll be in the sitting room."

Sir emerged a short while later, his muscular body encased in a gaudy brocade robe in brilliant hues of scarlet and gold. "It's a gift from my maternal grandmother," he explained when he caught Anthony's amazed look. "She's one of my few remaining relations who still admits to my existence."

Anthony said nothing, watching as Sir settled in one of the shabby chairs facing the fireplace. He knew Sir's break with his family was part of a carefully constructed charade, but he wondered how he could live with the censure of society. He hoped that in similar circumstances he would be equally as courageous.

A giggling maid with a generous display of bosom showing over the low-cut bodice of her gown appeared with the tea tray. After winking and flirting with them to no avail she flounced from the room, her broad hips swaying provocatively beneath her skirts. Anthony paid her no mind, a frown marring his forehead as he stared down at the chipped, cracked cups and the paltry assortment of breads and cheeses. He couldn't help but compare this repast to the sumptuous tea he had enjoyed at the Shiptons'. His frown deepened as he remembered Miss Malvern's impassioned defense of the Luddites, and he wondered if any of them would find fault with the simple meal.

"My apologies for the food," Sir drawled, noting Anthony's expression. "But at least it's hot. You must have bribed Mrs. Ferris."

"I gave her two shillings, actually." Anthony poured a cup of tea and handed it to him. "And I assure you, there's nothing wrong with the meal. I was merely thinking."

"About Shipton?" Sir accepted the cup and selection of food. "You're certain he's our man? Or"

—a rare smile lit his sea-blue eyes—"perhaps I should say our lady?"

"He's Lady X," Anthony replied staunchly. "I'm convinced of it."

"You'll forgive me if I appear somewhat dubious," Sir continued, wincing at the watery taste of the inferior tea. "But I have known the man for years, and he's a damned boor. I find it difficult to believe he is responsible for the *Journals.* The treasonous passages aside, they are most cleverly written, and clever has never been a word one would associate with the Earl of Shipton."

"Perhaps not," Anthony conceded, unperturbed by his superior's cautious attitude. Given the serious nature of their suspicions, he knew they would have to be certain of their proof before making their move. If they were wrong, they risked not only ruining an innocent man but allowing the real traitor to escape as well. "But Shipton *is* Lady X."

"Tell me again why you suspect him," Sir said quietly, his eyes resting on Anthony's face.

Anthony rose from his chair and began pacing the narrow confines of the crowded room. He paused in front of the dirt-encrusted window, staring down at the teeming street below. "The earl has been living well above his means for the past several years," he said without inflection. "And it is well known that he's been selling off portions of the estate not entailed to his son. In fact, until quite recently the rumor was that he was deep in dun territory, and would have to flee the country if he wished to avoid a financial scandal."

"That is true of half the lords in Parliament," Sir replied. "But's hardly enough to convict a man of treason."

"True," Anthony agreed, turning to face Sir. "But two years ago the earl suddenly came into a rather large amount of money which he claims he inherited from a distant relation who had recently died."

"Am I to take it no such relation existed?"

"None that I can find any trace of, and, believe me, I searched." Anthony added grimly, "The same thing happened less than a year ago, and again, no trace of this generous relation can be found. And the amounts are far from trifling. The last bit of money he came into was in excess of ten thousand pounds."

Sir gave a soundless whistle. "That is rather interesting. I wish my relations would be half so obliging." He took a sip of tea. "Perhaps Shipton gambles."

"He does, but not to any noticeable degree of success. I stole a peek at the books at White's, and although he hasn't lost any great sums, he does seem to lose with astonishing regularity. One wonders why he doesn't take up a more profitable and pleasurable pastime," Anthony added with a sardonic grin.

"Speaking of which, does he have a mistress?" Sir asked, helping himself to some of the bread and cheese. "Although I must own I can't imagine that formidable wife of his letting him off the string long enough to dally with a member of the muslin company."

Anthony's eyes took on a deadly shine. "Oh, he has a mistress, all right," he said softly. "One Madame Daphne Bouchett. Recognize the name?"

"I've seen it on some of the reports." Sir rubbed a finger across his lip. "A low-level courier, no?"

"Among other things," Anthony agreed. "She keeps a house in Belgravia that is known to attract some . . . shall we say . . . persons of interest to us? And she has been his mistress only since the convenient death of this alleged relation."

"How often does he visit her?"

"At least twice a week," Anthony said, resuming his seat and staring thoughtfully into the cold grate. "But never the same nights. I've set a man to watch the house and keep track of him for the next few weeks."

"Excellent." Sir looked pleased. "Report back to me if you learn anything more of value. We'll need more than this to convince the Regent."

"Shipton is . . . or rather, was, a member of the Privy Council," Anthony continued. "And much of the information given in the *Journals* was discussed in at least one of those meetings."

"That's it, then." Sir set his plate aside, his expression harsh. "Good job, Marchfield, you have built a very strong case against the earl. Do you want me to arrange for him to be taken into custody?"

Anthony paused, staring down at his clenched hands. "Not just yet," he said quietly. "We have proof he may well be a traitor, but there is nothing yet that proves he is Lady X. Since we do not want to tip the frogs off by directly approaching the publisher and demanding he give us Lady X's true identity, I think it best if we hold off for now. Until I have the evidence I need."

"And what evidence might that be?"

"Copies of the *Journals* written in Lady X's own hand, of course."

Sir raised a gold eyebrow. "Do you have such copies?" he asked in a quiet voice.

"Not yet," Anthony admitted, "but I know where they might be. Lady Shipton let it slip that the earl keeps whatever it is he's been writing locked up in his desk drawer. I hope to get a look at them before the end of the week."

"Do you anticipate any problems?"

Anthony's lips twisted in a sardonic grin as he remembered Lady Shipton's fawning farewell. She had all but handed him the keys to the house in order to ensure he would pay a return visit. "None," he answered confidently. "Lady Cassandra and I are to drive out tomorrow, in fact. Perhaps if I arrive early enough I might even have a peek then."

"Don't be overly hasty," Sir cautioned. "If Shipton is Lady X, we don't want to tip him off by making our move before everyone is in position. Just concentrate on worming yourself into the family's confidence, and we'll go from there."

"Yes, Sir."

"Very good, Marchfield," Sir nodded his approval. "In the meanwhile, I think we should limit our contact. There is too much at stake to risk exposure of the entire operation in the event you are discovered."

"As you say, Sir," Anthony replied, flicking a puzzled glance at his commander. In all the years he had worked for Sir he had never known him to give such an order without very good cause. "May I ask why?" he asked in a curious voice.

Sir shrugged his shoulders, rising to his feet to pace as Anthony had done earlier. "It may be nothing," he said slowly, his expression brooding. "But there have been some . . . rather puzzling problems developing with some of our other operatives in the past few weeks. Two have failed to keep their rendezvous, and the third was found dead in his lodgings a few days ago."

"Murdered?" Anthony tensed warily, his hands balling into fists. Violent death was an inevitable part of his chosen profession, but it was never something he could accept with equanimity.

"A bad heart, at least that is how the drunken sot of a physician would have it," Sir answered, his eyes flashing with fury and pain. "But I have my doubts; Jeffries wasn't a day above forty, and his health was excellent as far as any of us knew."

Anthony flinched. Adam Jeffries was an old friend who had joined Sir's men after losing an arm in battle. Anthony himself had recruited him. "Do you have any suspects?" he asked, his voice unnaturally calm.

"A few." Sir gave him a wary look. "But whoever it is, Marchfield, *I* will handle him. Vengeance is a commodity we can ill afford in this business. Do you understand me?"

"Yes, Sir," Anthony replied, struggling to control his emotions. "But it's hard, damned hard."

"I know," Sir said in an understanding tone. "But we have no other choice, Anthony. For now, the important thing is that Lady X be stopped."

Chapter Three

The news that Cassandra would be driving out with the duke on the following morning threw Lady Shipton into a positive frenzy of activity. The duke's barouche had barely disappeared around the corner before she was issuing orders like a general preparing for battle. Jacinda was hastily summoned back to the parlor for the council of war.

"Cassandra, dearest, I want you to go right upstairs and try on your new carriage dress!" the countess ordered, pacing about the room. "We must make certain it is exactly right. Jacinda, please write a note to my aunt Millicent and ask her to come here at once!"

"Lady Tarryville, Aunt?" Jacinda queried hesitantly, shooting Lady Shipton a puzzled look. "Are you quite certain? She is a dear lady, of course, but there's no denying the fact that she is a trifle . . . er . . . eccentric.''

"Really, Jacinda, must you be so difficult?'' The countess glared at her angrily. "I'm perfectly aware that my aunt's mental faculties are not what they should be, but that hardly signifies. I simply want her to chaperon Cassandra and the duke on their ride. They can hardly ride about unaccompanied,'' she added somewhat waspishly.

"I realize that, ma'am,'' Jacinda said, keeping her voice level with a conscious will. "But I fail to see why we must bother her ladyship. I have always acted as Cassie's chaperon whenever one was needed, and although I've no wish to go riding up and down the already crowded streets, I'm more than willing to do my duty.''

"How noble of you, I am sure,'' her aunt retorted with a sniff. "But you must know it would never answer. You hardly have either the ton or the position to provide adequate protection from the gossips once it becomes known my baby has fixed the duke's interest.''

"Why?''

"Because, simpleton, he is a *duke!*'' Lady Shipton snapped, vexed beyond all endurance by Jacinda's ignorance. "If Marchfield were a mere viscount or even an earl I suppose you would suffice, but when one is dealing with a duke, well, certain precautions must be taken. My daughter's reputation must be preserved at all costs, and if I let her go racketing about with Marchfield without at least a peeress in the carriage with them,

everyone will say that she is on the catch for
him!"

"But she is on the catch for him!" Jacinda protested. The strictures of society were even more
idiotic than she had first supposed, and after four
years she was no closer to understanding them.

Her aunt drew herself erect at this implied slur
on her daughter's character. "My Cassandra," she
announced in her most forbidding tones, "is the
daughter of an earl, and the granddaughter of the
Duke of St. Greeves. Marchfield may count himself quite fortunate that we would even consider
an alliance with his family. After all, his title only
dates back to the first George, while our family
may trace its line back to the time of Henry the
Seventh!"

"But—"

"Write the note, Jacinda," her aunt sighed, laying the back of her hand on her forehead. "I vow,
you have quite given me the headache!"

Jacinda judiciously took her leave, going to her
aunt's study for some paper. She drafted the required note, then gave it to the footman, telling
him with a wink to hurry and deliver it as it was
a matter of the greatest urgency.

"That I'll do, Miss Jacinda," he responded with
a cheeky grin. "I heard her ladyship a'squawkin',
and I reckon I know when to make myself
scarce!"

"Just be sure the note gets delivered," she said,
her mouth lifting in a rueful smile. She wondered
if her aunt and uncle were aware of the way their
antics were discussed below stairs; not that she
intended telling them, of course. The servants

had proven to be a great source of information, and much of what they told her had found its way into the *Journals*.

Her duty to her family accomplished, she went up to the library to begin her day's work. After retrieving the notebook from the shelf, she sat down and reviewed what she had written yesterday. The fourth journal was taking shape nicely, and she was certain that the character of Lord Stiffback would give her book that wonderful touch of malice for which Lady X was so justly famous. At least she thought he would.

Her forehead pleated as she recalled her conversation that morning with the Duke of Marchfield. At first she had been satisfied that he was a complete boor: priggish, self-righteous, and as insufferably proud as a prince. But when he had praised her, and then defended her against her aunt, she didn't know quite what to make of him. The man was a complete enigma, and she detested enigmas.

Her hazel eyes took on a thoughtful glow as she rested her chin in her hand. Perhaps she was becoming cynical, she brooded, staring at the framed portrait of her granduncle that adorned the far wall. She had been out in society for four years now, and that was enough to affect anyone's sensibilities! Still, there was something in Marchfield's proud carriage and cold gray eyes that set him apart from other men. It was as if he were always passing judgment on those about him, and such pretentiousness fairly cried out for parody.

She was merely holding up a mirror to society,

she told herself. If they didn't like what they saw, well, that was hardly *her* fault. Besides, satire was an acceptable form of social comment; one had only to read *Utopia* or *Pilgrim's Progress* to realize that.

As a writer it was her responsibility to expose life about her, and there was nothing wrong in that. Nothing at all. Feeling somewhat mollified, she bent her head over her notebook and began writing furiously.

The family was dining out that evening at the home of Lord Broadmoore, a pompous Tory whom Jacinda cheerfully loathed. He had appeared in the first book as Lord Boormore, and she had taken malicious pleasure in knowing that he had bribed her publisher in an unsuccessful effort to learn her identity. Her uncle was to accompany them, but at the last minute he cried off, claiming a sudden emergency.

"What sort of emergency?" her aunt demanded, eyeing him with marked suspicion.

"A governmental emergency, my love," Lord Shipton replied, stuffing the note a footman had brought him into the pocket of his claret velvet jacket. "Nothing you need to worry about. I'll join you as quickly as I can, I promise you." And he scurried away, shouting for the footman to summon him a coach.

"I suppose we ought to be grateful he left us the carriage," Lady Shipton grumbled, flinging herself against the plush velvet squabs and folding her arms across her chest. "I shudder to think of the talk it would have caused if we had arrived at the marquess's in a *rented* hack."

"Well, it's very disobliging of Papa, if you ask me," Cassandra said with a pout, pulling her velvet cloak about her. It was the same soft white as her silk evening gown, and trimmed with matching gold braid. She was wearing dangling ear bobs of gold and diamonds, and with her dark hair curled in the latest style she looked like an exotic princess. "Now Lord Broadmoore will expect us to entertain him," she added, her brown eyes flashing with resentment.

"Yes, and unfortunately we dare not ask Jacinda to keep him occupied," Lady Shipton sighed, giving Jacinda a pointed look. "She will only say some foolish thing to set him off, and then he'll spend the rest of the evening spouting politics at us!"

"I'm sorry, Aunt Prudence," Jacinda murmured, grateful the darkness of the carriage hid her smug smile. "I truly didn't mean to upset his lordship. How was I to know he would feel so strongly about the Catholic question?"

The older woman's lips thinned with disapproval. "A *lady*," she stressed the title with cutting irony, "would never presume to have anything so unfeminine as an opinion. Still, I suppose it's not entirely your fault," she added with a heavy sigh. "You are a bluestocking."

"Thank you for your understanding, Aunt," Jacinda replied, amused by her aunt's tone of voice. One would think she suffered from a fatal disorder, she thought, turning her head to gaze out the carriage window. According to Lady

Shipton's dicta, for a female the only suitable topics of conversation were the intricacies of fashion or the weather. And gossip, of course, she amended, tucking a stray curl back into her chignon. Her aunt adored gossip, and fortunately for Lady X, she was an acknowledged master of the art.

Lord Broadmoore's town house was situated in Mayfair, and following the fashion he had invited several more guests than could be comfortably accommodated in its small rooms. After surrendering their wraps to the maid, they made their way to where their host and hostess were receiving their guests. Lady Shipton and Cassandra were greeted with every evidence of pleasure, while Jacinda was subjected to a wary scrutiny.

"Miss Malvern," the marquess muttered, bobbing a stiff bow. "Happy to see you."

"Your Lordship, my lady." Jacinda curtsied politely. She noted the marquess's cautious look, and wondered if she should reassure him. Lady X had her faults, but attacking her prey in their own home was not one of them; unless sufficiently provoked, of course.

"But where is your husband?" the marquess demanded of Lady Shipton. "Told me he would be here tonight."

"An unexpected emergency, my lord," Lady Shipton answered, unfurling her blue and white ostrich-plumed fan in a languid fashion. "As a loyal servant of His Highness, I'm sure you understand."

"Of course, of course." Lord Broadmoore nodded sagely. "Heard there was a bit of a flap at

Carlton House; the princess, don't you know.
Well, I'm sure I know when to hold my tongue.
Never know who might be listening, eh?" And he
laughed at his own witticism.

Once the social niceties had been dispensed
with, Lady Shipton and Cassandra hurried into
the salon, leaving Jacinda to fend for herself.
While her cousin concentrated on flirting with all
the eligible men, she drifted from group to group,
hoping to learn what she could of the princess's
latest peccadillo. The Princess of Wales usually
did such an excellent job of satirizing herself that
Lady X had no reason to include her in a journal,
but that didn't mean she was averse to hearing a
bit of juicy gossip.

She settled in her corner beside a large potted
palm, listening shamelessly to a group of white-
clad debs who were cynically discussing the mer-
its of various suitors. Suddenly one of the girls,
who reminded Jacinda of Cassie at her most unpleasant, broke out into light laughter.

"Well, I wouldn't waste my time if I were you,
Cynthia," she advised mockingly, her blue eyes
studying the other girl with obvious amusement.
"Reginald's regiment is about to be called up, and
it could be months before you see him again . . .
if ever."

"How do you know this?" a baby-faced blonde
demanded, her delicately tinted lips thrusting
forward in a pout. "I think you're making it up
out of spite!"

"Think what you like," the saucy-eyed brunette sniffed, looking maddeningly superior. "But
my brother is the colonel's aide, and I heard him

tell Mama that he would be leaving for the Continent within a month."

"Oh." The blonde looked crestfallen. "I'd forgotten Elliott was in uniform. But you're quite right, Deirdre; I shan't accept Reginald's suit after all. A fiancé is quite useless if he's never about to escort one to balls."

Such a callous attitude toward a young man who would soon be fighting and, God forbid, dying for his country, struck Jacinda as barbaric beyond belief, and she decided to include it in her journal. It would be interesting to see the little blonde's expression when she saw the conversation set down in its entirety in the next installment of Lady X, although she doubted the tiresome creature would have the sensitivity to recognize the inherent cruelty in her actions. That kind never did.

She spent the next half hour sitting quietly in her corner, hearing enough gossip and scandal to keep her scribbling for the next several days. Just as she was about to wander into the game room, she became aware of somebody watching her. Puzzled, she turned toward the door, her gaze meeting that of an elegantly dressed man with light brown hair. He raised his glass of champagne in acknowledgment, and then began edging his way through the crowd to reach her side.

"Good evening, Miss Malvern," Lord Jonathan Grayson, the younger son of the Duke of Lynstead, said, the smile on his handsome face not quite reaching his amber-colored eyes. "I heard you and your family would be dining here tonight. I trust you are all well?"

"Quite well, sir, I thank you," Jacinda answered, taking in his sartorial appearance with interest. He was dressed in an exquisitely cut jacket of cream satin that matched his silk evening breeches, and his cravat was arranged in the intricate folds of the Oriental. He wore several fobs suspended from his striped waistcoat, and no fewer than four rings adorned his slender fingers. Not quite a dandy, she decided with an amused smile, but a trifle too refined for her tastes. Cassandra would doubtlessly find him enchanting.

"I saw your aunt and lovely cousin in the salon," Lord Jonathan continued, not seeming to notice her careful study of him. "When I didn't see your uncle, I thought perhaps he might be in here with you."

"Unfortunately not, my lord," she answered carefully, wondering why Lord Jonathan should think her uncle would be in her company. "He had a last-minute change of plans, and was unable to attend."

"Pity," Lord Jonathan sighed, looking suitably regretful. "I was rather hoping to speak with him about that new filly of his. I hear she's a real sweet goer."

"Lady Fortune?" Jacinda brightened at the mention of the earl's prize Thoroughbred. Although not an accomplished rider she adored horses, and the blood-bay filly was one of her favorites. "I didn't know you were interested in horses, Lord Jonathan," she ventured uncertainly.

"All Englishmen are interested in horses, Miss Malvern," he replied, feigning indignation.

"Surely you know it is our national passion. But actually," he said, breaking into a reluctant smile, "it is my brother, the new duke, who is interested in Lady Fortune. He is hoping I might persuade Lord Shipton to sell her."

"Oh, dear," Jacinda said, frowning thoughtfully, "I'm certain my uncle will refuse. I heard him telling the Duke of Marchfield only this morning that he intends to race her a few more seasons before retiring her."

"Indeed?" Lord Jonathan frowned in brief consternation. "Well, I can't say that I blame him; I've heard she's won several purses already. Ah, well. Marcus will be disappointed, but I daresay he'll recover." He turned his light brown eyes on her. "Did I hear you say your uncle was speaking with Marchfield? I had no idea the two were even acquainted."

"They were introduced by the Countess Dechiens," Jacinda explained, surprised by his interest, for Lord Jonathan was but a casual acquaintance of her uncle's. "And his grace stopped by early this morning to pay his respects to my cousin and aunt."

"Did he now?" Lord Jonathan's lips twisted in an unpleasant sneer. "Well, that explains why he and Lady Cassandra are enjoying such a comfortable coze in the other room. A fast worker, is our duke."

"His grace is here tonight?" Jacinda blinked in surprise. She recalled her aunt mentioning the dinner invitation to the duke, but he'd given no indication that he'd be attending. How very odd, she mused.

"Oh, yes." Lord Jonathan raised his glass to his lips. " 'Tis said he applied some rather effective pressure on the marquess to acquire the last-minute invitation. At the time I wondered why he bothered, for Broadmoore hardly travels in the same circle as the illustrious Duke of Marchfield, but after seeing your beautiful cousin again, I can understand his determination. She is a diamond of the first water."

Jacinda made the appropriate noises, although privately she shook her head at the foibles of the masculine mind. Cassie was a beauty, there was no denying that, but she was also an arch shrew with a petulant nature and a cutting tongue. It made little sense to her that a man would be willing to overlook so sour a disposition merely because its owner was possessed of a fine, white complexion, raven-black tresses, and flashing dark eyes. Ah, well, she dismissed the matter from her mind, caveat emptor, as the Greeks would say.

"Of course," Lord Jonathan continued, eyeing her over the rim of his glass, "given Marchfield's current difficulty, I shouldn't wonder that he is courting your cousin. Lady Cassandra is eminently suitable for our noble duke."

"Is she?" Jacinda noted the barely suppressed resentment in his voice whenever he mentioned the duke, and was curious enough to ask, "Are you acquainted with his grace, Lord Jonathan? You seem to know him quite well."

"We share a mutual friend," he replied with an enigmatic smile, his light brown eyes moving over Jacinda's face. "But tell me, Miss Malvern, perhaps you would be good enough to answer a question for me." He stepped closer, his deep voice lowering to an intimate pitch. "Is it true your uncle is considering resigning his position on the Privy Council?"

Years of experience hiding her true emotions kept Jacinda from gasping at the question. She had heard her aunt and uncle discuss the possibility several times, but she didn't feel it was any of Lord Jonathan's business. Drawing herself up, she fixed him with a cool look.

"My uncle never discusses the crown's affairs at home, Lord Jonathan," she said, dismissing from her mind the countless times she had heard him discuss everything from troop appointments to the king's failing health. "If you have any questions on the matter, perhaps it might be best if you were to speak with him."

"Of course, Miss Malvern," Lord Jonathan replied with a courtly bow. "And I meant no offense, I assure you. I was merely wondering if that possibility might have something to do with Lord Marchfield's interest in Lady Cassandra, which, you must own, is rather sudden. It's well known he's had his eye on an important post for a number of years."

Again Jacinda was aware of the hidden animosity in Lord Jonathan's words. She recalled his saying that he and the duke shared a mutual "friend," and she wondered if that friend might be a woman; a ladybird, perhaps. She'd noticed a sarcastic edge in the way he had made the remark. Evidently he had lost his *chère amie* to the other man. She shot him a curious look. "Is that what you meant by Lord Marchfield's 'difficulty'?" she asked bluntly, deciding to turn the tables on him.

"In a way." He seemed more amused than annoyed at her tactics. "His father was a member of the king's Privy Council for many years, and Marchfield has hoped to follow in his footsteps. Unfortunately, the prince seems to have taken him into dislike, and without the proper endorsement . . ." He shrugged eloquently. "However, the 'difficulty' I alluded to is the pressure his family has been putting on him to take a proper wife and settle down. The betting at the club was that he would bow to their wishes and marry within the year. Marchfield is rather known for his strong sense of duty."

Jacinda could readily believe this; the duke struck her as the type who would do his duty or die in the attempt. No wonder Prinny didn't care for him, she thought, her hazel eyes dancing with secret amusement.

Lord Jonathan lingered a few more minutes before excusing himself. Watching him walk away, she debated whether or not she should use the information he had given her regarding Lord Marchfield. If the gentlemen were betting as to whether or not the duke would give in to his family's desire and marry, then she would use it in her next journal. It would be rather amusing to depict the pompous Lord Stiffback being dragooned into marriage by a group of hen-pecking female relations.

Dinner was a sumptuous repast that began with a selection of French potages, and ended with a towering chocolate mousse. In between the many courses there were several wines and champagnes to choose from, and Jacinda was happy to note that most of the fifty-odd guests were well on their way to becoming intoxicated.

Her dinner partner, an army captain home on leave, was certainly bosky. He had succeeded in maneuvering her out onto the terrace, and despite the fact they could be easily seen from the salon, she was having the greatest difficulty keeping him from pawing her. She was toying with the idea of emptying her glass of sherry on his fine uniform when the sound of someone clearing his throat caused the captain to raise his head.

"Good evening, Miss Malvern," Marchfield said, his cold gray eyes fastening themselves on the young officer. "I would be happy to escort you into the music room."

"Thank you, Your Grace." Jacinda was so relieved at being rescued from what was promising to be another embarrassing "accident" that she flashed the duke her most brilliant smile. "I should be happy to accompany you. Allow me to introduce you to my dinner partner, Captain Marcus Allsworth."

"Captain." Anthony didn't bother with the formalities, his eyes narrowing at the sight of the young captain's arm still resting with familiarity around Miss Malvern's waist. He had watched her fending off the young puppy's advances for several minutes before deciding to rescue her. It was obvious that she had no idea how to handle men, and he wondered why her family didn't keep a better eye on her.

"Your . . . Your Grace," Captain Allsworth stammered, his ruddy complexion becoming even more pronounced under the duke's cold perusal. As if realizing the reason behind that unwavering glare he stepped away from Jacinda, his arm dropping to his side. "I'm most honored to make your acquaintance."

"You're in the Ninety-fifth Regiment, aren't you?" Anthony asked, recognizing the soldier's green uniform.

"Yes, Your Grace," Captain Allsworth answered, running a tongue over his thick lips. There was a sense of danger emanating from the duke that made him shift uncomfortably, and he wondered anxiously if the duke's skill with a sword was as deadly as it was reputed to be.

"And your commanding officer is Colonel Bridgeway, is it not?" Anthony demanded, pleased to see that the captain wasn't so besotted with drink as to have lost his common sense. He knew he could be intimidating when he chose, and at the moment he chose to be extremely intimidating. He wanted it driven home to the young officer that Miss Malvern was not without some form of masculine protection.

"Y . . . yes, sir . . . Your Grace," Captain Allsworth replied, fighting the urge to turn tail and flee from the danger evident in the older man's soft voice and icy stare. Good gad, how was he to know that the silly chit he had been trying to kiss was possessed of so murderous a guardian? "Are . . . are you acquainted with the colonel, sir?" he asked, hoping to escape with his skin still intact.

"Quite well." Anthony smiled coldly. "I shall be sure to mention you to him the next time we meet. You may go now, Captain."

Paling at the threat in Anthony's words, the captain executed a quick bow, then departed, his medals and dress sword clanking in his haste. Jacinda watched him go, her lips curving in a delighted smile as she turned to face Marchfield.

"Let us hope our troops aren't so easily intimidated on the battlefield, Your Grace," she told him with a husky laugh. "I shudder to think of England's fate were such the case."

"It is your own fate, or rather, your own reputation that should most concern you at this moment, Miss Malvern," Anthony informed her, his anger transferring itself to her. He could scarcely believe she would be so foolish as to place herself in so untenable a position, and he meant to ensure that she never repeated her error. If her uncle lacked the will to control her behavior, then he would have to attend to the matter himself. With so much at stake, he simply couldn't afford the scrutiny a scandal would cause.

"I . . . I beg your pardon, Your Grace?" Jacinda asked, her smile fading at his harsh words.

"It was foolish beyond permission for you to come out here with Allsworth, Miss Malvern," he continued coolly, staring down the length of his nose at her. "I wasn't the only person who witnessed your shocking behavior with the captain, and you may be quite sure it will cause some very unpleasant speculation. Were I you, ma'am, I should have greater care of my reputation."

"And were I you, Your Grace, I should not have found myself dragged out onto the balcony and pawed by a drunken soldier!" Jacinda shot back, scarcely believing the duke would dare attack her for something that was clearly not her fault. Her earlier doubts about him vanished in her quick flare of temper, and she vowed to make him pay for his perfidy. Lord Stiffback was worse than a prig, she decided, her hands clenching in rage as she glared at him; he was a bullying, meddlesome bore!

Jacinda's response made Anthony stiffen in resentment. Here he had gone to the effort to rescue the silly chit from a dangerous situation, and rather than thanking him, she gave him a setdown. His black brows snapped together as he drew himself up to his full height, his muscular shoulders straining against the rich blue of his satin jacket.

"If you wish to avoid similar occurrences in the future, Miss Malvern, might I suggest you learn to adopt a more circumspect attitude? That way your actions are less likely to be . . . misinterpreted." He added the last word with mocking delicacy.

Jacinda was speechless at such arrogance. In an effort to regain her temper, she glanced past the duke's broad shoulders, her eyes falling on the glass of sherry she had set down when the captain had first taken her into his arms. She stared at it, an evil plan forming quickly in her mind. Her glance snapped back to Marchfield's face, and she managed a slow smile.

"And if I should . . . inadvertently find myself in the same predicament—alone on a balcony with some overwrought man who has misunderstood my actions—would you say I was justified in doing whatever it took to free myself?" she asked in her sweetest tones, moving carefully around the duke until she could feel the cool glass with her fingertips.

Anthony considered the matter for a moment. "Short of sticking a knife in the scoundrel, I suppose it would be understandable if you did what was necessary to win your freedom," he replied calmly, hiding a smile at the image of Miss Malvern slapping her assailant across the face. Despite surface appearances he was learning she could be a tigress, and doubtlessly she would give a good accounting of herself if cornered. The notion pleased him for some unknown reason.

"Then you would approve of such actions?" Jacinda pressed, her fingers tightening around the stem of the glass. "You wouldn't be angry?"

"Not at all," he assured her with a magnanimous smile. "I would understand completely."

"I'm very glad to hear that, my lord," she cooed, beaming at him beatifically before tossing the contents of the glass in his face.

Without waiting for his reaction, she turned and fled from the balcony. It took her only a few minutes to find her aunt, who was sitting in the salon holding forth with a group of her old cronies. She waited patiently until the chair beside the countess was vacant before sitting down.

"Why, Jacinda, whatever is the matter?" Lady Shipton demanded, taking in Jacinda's flushed face and downcast eyes with concern. "Are you ill?"

"Oh, no, Aunt," she assured the countess. "But I'm afraid you're going to be quite angry with me. You see, there's been another unfortunate accident. . . ."

Chapter Four

Jacinda spent the next week in disgrace. When the Duke of Marchfield returned from the balcony with a wet face and a ruined jacket, pandemonium had erupted around her. Once they had reached the safety of their home her aunt sobbed and threatened to swoon, Cassandra raged and called her a graceless idiot, and the earl hinted broadly that perhaps it was time she was fitted for a pair of spectacles. Jacinda weathered the storm with her customary show of penitence, hiding in the library until she felt it was safe to come out again.

She spent the time working on her book, adding at least another fifty pages to the existing manuscript. Lord Stiffback now dominated the book, and she considered him to be her best character to date. He was wonderfully masterful: arrogant and overbearing, dictating the behavior of others with the smug superiority of a pontiff. Upon reflection she gave him a slight stammer, deciding it made his pompous speeches that much more annoying. She also gifted him with a hectoring mother, who followed him around reminding him to keep his coat fastened and to stay out of drafts.

Her uncle confirmed that there were indeed bets on the books as to whether or not the duke would take a wife, although he cautioned her not to repeat the story. As she considered the earl to be an impeccable source she included the tale, giving it the special touch her readers expected. But even after all the work she had done on the character, she still felt it needed fleshing out, and once her self-imposed exile was ended, she set about to correct the deficiency.

Marchfield cooperated in that he was now an almost daily visitor, a fact that had Cassandra and Lady Shipton almost giddy with triumph. They seemed to take his calls as some sort of declaration, which amused Jacinda no end. But when they began discussing wedding gowns, she felt compelled to speak up.

"Really, cousin," she drawled, adding another row of stitches to her sampler, "aren't you being a trifle premature? The duke hasn't even made an offer as yet."

"That shows you how much *you* know!" Cassandra retorted, her cheeks as rosy as her morning gown. "He's asked me to two balls this past week alone, and he's hinted he shall be desolate when I leave London!"

"Ah, I apologize then," Jacinda said, setting her sewing to one side. "I had no idea things had progressed so far." She rose to her feet, shaking the loose threads from the skirts of her flowered muslin gown. They were sitting in the morning parlor, enjoying a cup of tea in the soft sunlight streaming through the open drapes. The blue and rose parlor with its delicate Aubusson carpets and gilded Hepplewhite furniture was located in the rear of the house, and the soft scent of flowers drifted through the partially open doors. Jacinda crossed the room to stand before them, smiling at the sight of the bright flowers blooming in the tiny garden. It always amazed her that the fragile blossoms were able to survive in the filthy London air, and she admired their brave beauty.

"Well, there's more to it than that, of course," Lady Shipton said, helping herself to one of Cook's fresh strawberry tarts. "Last night at Almack's he stood up with her twice, and at the Fitzroys' musicale on Monday he sat beside her for the entire evening!"

"An offer in form, I agree." Jacinda laughed, returning to her overstuffed chair and picking up her discarded sampler. "Has anyone checked the *Gazette* to see if he has sent in an announcement?"

"Pray don't think you're being amusing, Jacinda," her aunt said, bending a disapproving frown on her. "Believe me, there is nothing more tiresome than a woman who considers herself to be clever. It's all that studying you do that's to blame, I expect," she sighed, lifting her teacup to her lips.

Jacinda drove the needle's sharp point through her finger. Flinching with pain, she stuck the injured finger in her mouth. "*What* did you say?" she mumbled, sucking on her finger.

"I said you spend entirely too much time closeted away with your studies," Lady Shipton replied with a frown. "After all, what earthly good is it? A gentleman wants a lady for a wife, not some clever little bluestocking who spends her days with her nose in a book! If you have any hopes at all of making a good marriage, my girl, you would do well to give up this nonsense."

Jacinda bent her head, hiding the resentment that flared through her at her aunt's words. She was the first to admit the *Journals* were frivolous, but to hear them dismissed as "nonsense" filled her with indignation.

Despite the *Journals'* unquestioned popularity, they were still considered quite scandalous by society, and she knew she would be ruined were she to claim authorship . . . even to her own family. Her uncle would no doubt order her from the house, and she would be destitute. The *Journals* were bringing in a good income, small but steady, and her publisher had promised her a substantial increase with the next book. If she was careful, she would be able to support herself quite comfortably; but not just yet. Until that day she had no choice but to bite her tongue, keeping her temper and her secret to herself.

Anthony divided his time between paying court to Lady Cassandra and worming his way into the earl's confidence in order to get a peek at the *Journals.* At the first he enjoyed an easy victory, though he was only moderately successful at the other. The earl was polite but cautious . . . almost too cautious to Anthony's way of thinking. It was his experience that an innocent man was as transparent as glass, and a guilty man was opaque, skillfully revealing only what he chose to reveal.

Acting like a well-heeled suitor investigating a potential father-in-law, he casually inquired into Shipton's finances. The earl put him off with the tale of deceased relatives who had left him all their worldly possessions. When Anthony pressed for greater detail the earl grew markedly uneasy, muttering something about "timely investments" before quickly changing the subject. After ten frustrating days he admitted he could learn no more, and out of desperation he set up a meeting with Sir in a less than elegant gaming establishment—something to which his superior took the greatest exception.

"I thought I told you to avoid all but the most necessary contact," he told Anthony, pretending to study the cards he had just been dealt. "We could be under observation even now."

"I realize that, Sir," Anthony apologized, shuffling his cards restlessly. "But I had no choice. Shipton is either the best agent I've ever encountered or he's as innocent as a nun at prayers. I've learned next to nothing."

"This is quite a volte-face," Sir drawled, raising a glass of amber-colored liquid to his lips and downing the contents in a single gulp. To an observer it would appear the well-dressed man in the bottle-green velvet jacket and white pantaloons was well on his way to becoming bosky, but in reality, the glass contained weak tea mixed with just enough brandy to scent his breath.

"When you last reported in, you all but had the final plank nailed into the earl's scaffold. Why the change of heart?"

Anthony sunk lower in his rickety chair, staring thoughtfully at the group of men clustered around a faro table. "I haven't changed my opinion . . . exactly," he said, raising his glass to his lips. "I'm convinced the man is Lady X, but I haven't been able to prove a damned thing."

"Have you seen the *Journals*?" Sir asked. Like Anthony he had noticed the four men, and was watching them through narrowed blue eyes.

"Not as yet," Anthony admitted grimly. "Lady Shipton keeps me confined to the parlor, and I haven't had the chance to search the earl's study. The season won't end for several weeks yet, and I'm not certain I can maintain my subterfuge for that long."

"The role of ardent suitor is growing difficult, is it?" Sir drawled, shifting in his chair until his hand touched the handle of the small pistol he kept tucked in his waistcoat. Anthony saw the movement and automatically followed suit, his fingers curving around his own weapon. He had a second pistol hidden in his boot and a stiletto up one sleeve. He had not survived this long as one of Sir's agents without learning to guard against any eventuality.

"It's becoming extremely hazardous," he said, continuing with the conversation although he was alert to Sir's every move. They had set their cards down, and were now pretending to concentrate on their drinking. The four men at the other table kept playing faro, but Anthony noticed the man facing him had moved slightly, his face now in shadow. It could be coincidence, or it could be a trap, but judging from the way his scalp was tingling he rather suspected it was the latter. Taking another sip of his tea-brandy mixture, he spoke in a voice that was meant to be overheard.

"Yes, as I was saying, it is growing most tiresome. The last time I visited Lady Cassandra the countess hinted that the next time I came to call I bring my mother with me. 'Twould seem her ladyship has me pegged as her future son-in-law. Can you imagine such brass?"

"I can indeed, old fellow," Sir agreed, his voice also loud. "Well, in that case I can understand why your mind isn't on our little game. The very notion of matrimony is enough to give any man the blue devils. You had best tread lightly, however. The earl is a puffed-up old prig who won't look kindly upon you trifling with his daughter's affections. One wrong move and you could well find yourself leg-shackled to the baggage."

Anthony shuddered with mock horror. "Heaven forbid," he intoned piously, signaling for the barman to bring two more glasses. He could see the other men were definitely listening to their conversation, and it was important that they maintain the proper pose. There was no chance now of discussing anything of import with possible enemy agents sitting not six feet away from them. Yet it would look odd if they were to leave so soon. For now it was safest to remain where they were and see what the men would do.

"If you want my advice, you should avoid such

pretty little marriage traps as I do." Sir was content to follow Anthony's lead. "There are dozens of luscious females about to entertain oneself with, and you may rest assured none of them expects marriage as the price for their favors."

They spent the next half hour discussing women and drinking deeply. Their voices grew louder and their discussion increasingly coarse as they gave every appearance of two gentlemen out on the town. In the end it was Sir who decided they should leave, staggering to his feet as he announced he had had enough of the tavern's "swill."

"Come back to my place, ol' boy," he said, throwing his arm around Anthony's shoulders. "We shall share a bottle there, eh? Real French brandy, not this piss water." He swept the glasses off the table, turning to glare at the impassive barkeep. "And don't think I didn't notice you were watering your spirits, either!" he thundered, swaying slightly. "Won't ever come back again, either of us. Come along, Anthony. Can't stand the smell of this place a moment longer."

They stumbled outside, calling for a hack in loud voices and mutually abusing each other's parentage. Sir walked slightly ahead of Anthony, leading him in the direction of a darkened alleyway. The four men had followed them as he intended they should, and the attack, when it came, was easily dealt with.

The first two men went for Anthony, while the other two closed in on Sir. They were all large men, but they had been expecting their prey to be drunk, and therefore easy targets. When they found themselves suddenly facing two armed and sober men, they were at a loss as to what they should do.

Anthony took the first man down with a vicious kick to the groin, shoving him roughly aside as he grabbed the second man by the shoulders, throwing him headfirst into the stone wall. A quick blow to the back of his head sent the startled man into unconsciousness, and then he turned to help Sir, who had already dispatched one of his assailants with his fists. Together, they closed in on the remaining villain.

"I . . . now see here, guvs," the man stuttered in a thick cockney accent. "What's the problem, eh? You got no call to be threatenin' me an' my mates. We wasn't doin' nothin'."

"Indeed? You make it a habit to follow people down dark alleys, do you?" Sir inquired silkily, resting the blade of his knife against the man's fleshy throat.

"I . . . uh . . . well, ain't nothin' wrong liftin' a few purses, eh?" The man's eyes widened with fear, the whites gleaming palely in the meager light flickering from the single lantern at the entrance to the alley. "A man's got to live, don't he?"

"He does indeed." Sir leaned closer, the point of the knife nicking the man's filthy skin and drawing a thin welling of blood. "And if this man wants to live, he had best be prepared to answer a few questions. Who hired you?"

"Nobody!" the man cried, swallowing against the pain as the knife dug deeper into his flesh. "I swears it! Me an' my mates was goin' to relieve you of some of your blunt, that's all! Oh, please, sir, you're hurtin' me!"

"Who hired you?"

"A man . . . a gentleman . . . I don't know his name," he gasped, sweat pouring down his face. "He gave us a couple of quid each to make sure you learned your lesson is what he said. But that's all I know, sir, I swear on my mother's grave!"

"And were we slated to survive this 'lesson'?" Sir asked, relieving some of the pressure from the knife although he didn't release his grip on the man's dirt-stained jacket. While Sir waited for an answer Anthony bent and searched the other men's pockets, coming away with a crude assortment of weapons ranging from an ancient pistol to a piece of glass that had been honed to razor sharpness. He slipped them all into his pocket before turning his attention to the other man, searching him with cool expertise.

"Evidently not," he said, extracting a shiny new pistol from the man's pocket and handing it to Sir. "Look at his. Standard French army issue."

"French!" The man paled in horror. "Cor! As God's my witness, your honors, I don't know nothin' 'bout them frogs! The gentleman what hired us gave us that, in case you gave us a bit o' trouble. But he weren't French, sirs. He was English, he spoke like you! I wouldn't have nothin' to do with them French sons of . . ."

"What is your name?" Sir demanded.

"Jem Roberts, your honor."

"Well, Jem," Sir answered, releasing his hold on the man and taking a wary step away from him, "oddly enough I think I believe you. You may be a thief and a scoundrel, but I don't think you are a traitor."

"Never, sir!" Jem drew himself up proudly. "Me own brother died a'servin' his king, and I wouldn't never spit on his memory that a'way!"

"A commendable sentiment," Sir said sardonically. "A pity the man who hired you doesn't share it."

"He's a frog?"

"Worse, an Englishman who accepts French gold to betray his own countrymen." Anthony spoke softly, suspecting they might have an unexpected ally in their erstwhile attacker. "Would you recognize this 'gentleman' if you were to see him again?"

Jem used a filthy handkerchief to stem the flow of blood trickling down his chin. "That I would, guv!" he agreed with surprising cheerfulness. "He was a fine-lookin' bloke with brown hair and brown eyes. I remember he had a dandy fob I coulda gotten at least ten quid for down at McWarren's."

"What sort of fob?" Sir asked, his brow wrinkling in concentration.

"Gold, with a small diamond on the front . . . well, like that one, sir." And he pointed a grubby finger at the front of Sir's waistcoat.

"I see." Sir's words were soft. "If this gentleman should contact you again, Jem, I want you to do me a favor."

Jem drew himself up like a soldier about to receive his orders. "Anything, guv'nor!"

"I want you to go to the barkeep back at that

charming tavern we were just in, and tell him you
need to see me."

"That's all?" Jem looked somewhat crestfallen.

"That's more than enough, I promise you," Sir
assured him. "There are many, many lives at
stake here, *English* lives, and you can help us all if
you'll do this for me."

"I'd be proper proud to, sir!" Jem vowed, his
face fairly glowing with resolve. "You can count
on ol' Jem, and his mates," he added, gesturing at
the three men who were slowly stirring on the
ground.

"I would appreciate it." Sir smiled at Jem's
words. "And might I apologize for the slight mis-
understanding? I trust none of your men are
hurt?"

"Cor, sir, we usually get worse 'n this from our
wives!" Jem chuckled. "Think nothin' of it."

"You're too generous." Sir dug into the pocket
of his waistcoat, extracting a gold coin that he
flipped to Jem. "Something for your trouble," he
said, smiling as the man expertly caught the coin
in his fist. "I should hate for you and your men to
go home empty-handed."

Jem's eyes gleamed at the sovereign in his
hand. "Much obliged to you, guv. You and your
friend are real gentlemen, I can tell."

"Thank you." Sir bowed. "A gentleman always
appreciates being recognized by his fellows. I
shall be waiting to hear from you."

"Wait, guv!"

"Yes?"

"Well"—Jem shifted uneasily—"you said if I
was to see that other man again I should tell the

man at the tavern I needed to see you. But I can't rightly do that, can I?''

"Why not?" Sir queried.

"Well, sir, that's goin' to be hard to do, if I don't even know your name."

Sir broke out into a low chuckle. "You do know my name, Jem," he said gently. "In fact, you have been calling me it since we were first . . . er . . . introduced."

"Sir?" Jem was clearly puzzled.

"Precisely, Jem," came the soft reply. "Sir. Tell the barkeep you need to see Sir, and he will get word to me. Until then, Jem, I shall bid you farewell."

Anthony waited until they were securely bolted in Sir's rented rooms before turning to face him. "A traitor," he said grimly. "A traitor in our own group." He pulled out his fob that was the mate to the one Sir and his other operatives wore. "My God, I cannot believe it!"

"I wish I could say the same," Sir replied quietly, staring at his own fob with troubled eyes. "But I have long suspected as much."

"But who?" Anthony ran a hand through his black hair, adding to his disheveled appearance. "Our men are selected and trained by you! That one of them could turn against us . . . against you . . ." He shook his head in disbelief, his gray eyes snapping to Sir's face. "Any ideas?"

"Well, we know it's not either of us," Sir said, pouring a glass of brandy and handing it to Anthony. "You heard Jem; the man had brown hair and brown eyes. Unfortunately, about half my agents could fit that description, if not more." He poured a glass for himself as well, his expression somber as he raised the snifter to his lips.

Anthony took a mouthful of the fiery spirit, savoring its warmth. He was stunned. An agent could trust no one, not even lifelong friends when he was on assignment. He had to be prepared for danger and betrayal at every turn; it went with the dangers of the duty. But he should be able to trust and depend upon his fellow agents. Without that, he was completely alone, and he knew from experience that that was a very dangerous spot to be in.

"What are you going to do?" he asked quietly.

"Start looking," Sir replied in a tight voice. "I shall have to review the records of each agent. Somewhere, somehow, I must have missed something in their backgrounds. Naturally I shall have to inform the prince."

"Naturally," Anthony agreed, taking another sip of brandy, his mouth hardening as he considered the regent's probable reaction.

"I'll have to reassign several people," Sir continued, staring desolately out his window. "Cancel some plans. I dare not risk any agents on the Continent just now. It would be too dangerous."

"What about me? Should I abandon my search?"

"Not just yet," Sir decided after a careful pause. "You should be fairly safe for the moment as this assignment is just between you and me; not even His Highness is aware of what you are doing. If the situation changes, I'll contact you."

He took another sip of brandy. "How close do you think you are to finding the *Journals*?"

"I know they are in the earl's desk," Anthony answered carefully. "I will do my best to get a peek at them while I'm there visiting Lady Cassandra. But if need be, I suppose we could search the house at night while they are out."

"Too risky," Sir decided. "Servants have been known to take occasional shots at thieves, and if Shipton is Lady X the *Journals* are likely to be concealed in some inaccessible place. Besides, think of the embarrassment should you be caught in flagrante delicto."

"I've suffered worse embarrassments," Anthony assured him, warming to the idea of a clandestine visit. He found the earl and his lady to be boring beyond endurance, while Lady Cassandra's cloying smiles and simpering ways were growing increasingly hard to tolerate. The only member of the household he found bearable was Miss Malvern, and he wasn't even sure if he liked her. No, the more he thought of it, a simple break-in was the best answer. But first, he would have one final try during the day.

Chapter Five

Anthony was back at the Shiptons' early the following afternoon, determined to find the proof he wanted. Lady Shipton and Cassandra received him in the parlor, and after a few minutes of cordial pleasantries, he got down to business.

"I was hoping if I might have a word with your husband, my lady. Is he still at home?" he inquired politely, knowing full well the earl had left over an hour ago. Sir had a man stationed across the street monitoring the comings and goings of the household, and there wasn't much he didn't know about Shipton's movements. Now if they could just get a man posted inside . . .

"I'm terribly sorry, Your Grace, but he's already left for the day," Lady Shipton replied, chewing her bottom lip in obvious distress. "But if it's important, I can send a servant with a note to fetch him home."

Anthony hid a smile at the countess's patent eagerness. Evidently she was hoping he had come to ask the earl's permission to wed their daughter. His eyes flickered to Cassandra, noting her preening, self-satisfied expression with cool derision. It would appear both ladies were due for a severe disappointment.

"Please don't bother," he told the countess politely. "I only wished to question him about his investments."

"His investments?" Lady Shipton wasn't about to admit defeat just yet.

"Yes, he mentioned he's had some success with

his recent investments, and I'd hoped to discuss them with him," he replied, crossing his legs and flashing her a bland look. "Would you happen to know the name of his counselor?"

"Heavens, no!" Lady Shipton was hard-pressed to hide her disappointment. "Such masculine things are scarcely any of *my* concern, now are they?" she asked, fanning herself vigorously. "You mustn't think that I am one of those meddlesome wives who are forever sticking their noses into their husband's affairs. Indeed not! And I have raised my daughter not to do the same. Haven't I, dear one?" She gave her daughter a maternal smile.

"Yes, Mama," Cassandra simpered, fluttering her lashes at Anthony. "I'm sure *I* should never presume to tell my husband his duty." She was dressed in a pretty gown of striped-cream-and-cherry-colored jaconet muslin, trimmed with red ribbons about the high waistline and ruffled cuffs. The gown showed her dark hair and eyes and creamy shin to perfection, and Anthony had to admit she made a lovely picture.

But such domestic talk made him uneasy and he sought sanctuary in his tea, his sense of self-preservation overcoming his professional duties. But only temporarily. When he felt it safe to resume his line of questioning, he tried again.

"Do you think he might have the information in his study? I do hate to impose, but it is rather important. Perhaps if I were to check his desk . . ." His voice trailed off suggestively.

Lady Shipton hesitated, uncertain as to what she should do. She didn't wish to offend a highly eligible suitor for her daughter's hand, but neither did she wish to incur her husband's wrath by allowing another man to search through his personal belongings. In the end, it was fear of upsetting her husband that decided her.

"I'm very sorry, Your Grace," she said with visible reluctance, "but I'm afraid I simply can't allow it. My husband treasures his privacy. I'm sure you understand."

"Of course, my lady," he murmured, silently cursing the countess's sensibilities. The story he'd spun about wanting the counselor's name had been a shot in the dark; now he would have to think of something else. The only other alternative was to risk breaking into the house and locating the information by stealth—not the most reliable method of handling an investigation.

They spent the next half hour sipping tea and waiting for Lady Tarryville to join them. Anthony planned to take Cassandra for a drive about the park, and the elderly lady was needed to act as chaperon. When another twenty minutes passed with no sign of her, Lady Shipton decided to take action.

"Aunt must have forgotten your little outing," she said, turning a strained smile on Anthony. "The poor dear is rather old, and I fear she's grown shockingly forgetful."

"Oh, dear," Cassandra said with a pretty pout, "and I was so looking forward to our driving out. I have the loveliest new bonnet to show you, Your Grace, and I wanted you to see it." She gave her mother an anguished look. "Couldn't you come with us, Mama?"

"I'm afraid not, my angel," the countess sighed. "Lady Braxton is expecting me, and I simply can't cry off now." She laid a thoughtful finger on her lips as she contemplated the dilemma. "I know!" she cried at last. "Jacinda shall accompany you!"

"Mama, the very thing!" Cassandra cried, clapping her hands in delight. "I shall ring for the footman to go find her. She's probably in the library."

"Wait." Anthony stayed her hand as she reached for the bellpull. "I should be more than happy to go after her myself, my lady."

The countess blinked at his unexpected offer and the eagerness with which he made it. "I . . . well, that's very good of you, I am sure," she stammered. "But it's not necessary. We have servants aplenty; let them attend to it."

"Yes, but Miss Malvern was telling me of her collection of Hunt's latest essays." He spoke rapidly, improvising as he went along. This might be his only chance to escape Lady Shipton's eagle eye, and he meant to take it. "I was hoping to look at them the last time I was here, but there wasn't enough time. Unless Your Ladyship has some objection, that is?" He raised an eyebrow at her in silent challenge.

"Oh, my, no!" she assured him anxiously. "Please, Your Grace, you must consider my home your home. You are quite right, of course. Jacinda has added several volumes to my husband's collection, and you must feel free to borrow whatever you like." She tucked a stray curl back into her turban in a nervous gesture. "And might I say, sir, that you have shown remarkable generosity in forgiving my niece for her appalling clumsiness. I can't tell you how sorry I am for that most unfortunate incident."

"Accidents happen," Anthony soothed her, shutting out the image of the triumphant gleam in Miss Malvern's hazel eyes as she hurled the contents of her wineglass into his face. "Now if you'd be so good as to point me in the direction of the library, I shall go fetch our chaperon. I'm most eager to see your new bonnet gracing your lovely head," he added for good measure, shooting Cassandra a provocative look.

"It's on the next floor," Lady Shipton supplied, her words tripping over themselves in their eagerness to get out. "It's the first door on your right, directly across the hall from my husband's study."

Good, now he wouldn't have to go sneaking about the house like a light-fingered servant, Anthony thought, rising swiftly to his feet. After excusing himself with a low bow, he hurried from the room. He found the library with no trouble, and after casting the closed door a quick look, he opened the door to the study and slipped quietly inside.

The red and gold room was surprisingly small, the only furniture being the large cherry-wood desk and the gilded chair that was covered in the same gold damask as the heavy drapes. He quickly leafed through the papers piled on top of the desk, but finding nothing of interest, he turned his attention to the drawers. The top drawer was locked, but it took him less than ten seconds to open it with the thin metal blade he carried in his pocket. He slid the drawer open, a pleased smile spreading across his face at the sight of the neat stack of paper he found there. Glancing cautiously toward the door one final time, he picked up the first sheet of paper and began reading.

The sound of her uncle's door being opened brought Jacinda's head up in alarm. She had just finished her writing for the day and was reviewing her work, otherwise she might never have heard the soft sound. She set down her notebook, frowning at the door in consternation. "I wonder what he wants, Purrfect," she said, turning to the cat who was indolently sunning himself on the center of the table. "He never goes into his study in the middle of the day."

Purrfect flicked his bushy tail as if to indicate his supreme indifference to her question, and Jacinda glanced back at the door. "Perhaps I'd better see what he's doing," she decided. "He might be looking for something, and if he doesn't find it, he may take it in his head to come in here."

The thought of such a calamity drove her to her feet, and after tucking the notebook into its hiding place, she hurried across the hall. She found the door to the study standing partially ajar, and she pushed it open, a smile on her face as she stepped inside.

"Good afternoon, Uncle, I thought I heard . . ." Her voice trailed off as her eyes widened in shock. "Your Grace! Whatever are you doing here?"

Anthony's head jerked up at the sound of the door being opened, his hand reaching for his pistol. The sight of a wide-eyed Miss Malvern standing in the doorway surprised him, and for a moment he froze, remembering Sir's warning about being caught. At the time he had discarded the notion as improbable, but he hadn't reckoned with the unpredictable poor relation.

Thinking quickly, he returned the papers to the drawer, then stepped away from the desk, sliding the drawer closed with his finger. "Good afternoon, Miss Malvern," he said in what he hoped was an indifferent tone. "I've been looking for you."

"And naturally the first place you thought to check was my uncle's desk," Jacinda replied, her brows snapping together as she stepped into the room. "Well, I have news for you, Your Grace. That is not one of my customary hiding places."

Anthony's jaw tightened at her sharp words. Any other female would have taken his glib explanation at face value. If she took it in her head to tell her uncle she had found him snooping through his desk, then he was sunk. He decided it was safest for the moment to say nothing. If she did tattle to the earl, he had only to deny it. Something told him the Shiptons would be far more inclined to believe him than her.

"Lady Tarryville is unable to accompany your cousin and me on our drive," he said, walking toward her with studied nonchalance. "Your aunt requests that you join us to act as our chaperon."

"Does she?" Jacinda asked, wondering what she should do. For a brief moment she toyed with the notion of threatening to turn him over to her uncle, but in the end she decided against it. Besides, what could she say? That she had discovered the oh-so-proper Duke of Marchfield with his paws in the earl's desk? They would think her mad! And for all she knew, the dratted man had permission to be in the room. He certainly didn't *act* guilty, she brooded, studying him through her thick lashes.

Anthony returned her perusal with feigned indifference. His instincts told him that, for whatever reasons of her own, the meddlesome wench had decided to keep her own counsel, and he was quick to fortify his tenuous position. "I'll tell your aunt we may expect you in, say . . . fifteen minutes?" he inquired with a mocking drawl. "I'm sure that should give you enough time to change into something more . . . er . . . suitable."

Jacinda glanced down at her dress, momentarily distracted by his words. Although not in the first stare of fashion, the blue cambric gown with its high waist and ruffled bodice was quite stylish, and certainly more than suitable for a pleasant drive in the park. She opened her mouth to tell the duke as much, but he simply brushed past her, leaving the study without so much as a by-your-leave. It was only after he disappeared down the stairs that Jacinda realized he had adroitly sidestepped her question.

Clever, Your Grace, she thought, her eyes narrowing as she stared after him, very clever, indeed. His snide remark about her clothing had completely distracted her, allowing him to effect his escape unchallenged. It was a brilliant maneuver, and one she admired despite her annoyance. But if he thought this was the last of the matter, then he had sadly underestimated her . . . and Lady X. She turned toward her bedroom, her lips lifting in a wicked smile.

"I'm sorry if I kept you waiting, Aunt," she apologized some twenty minutes later as she entered the parlor. "But I'm ready to leave now."

"Well, 'tis about time!" Lady Shipton snapped, turning an impatient frown in Jacinda's direction. "It's already gone past four o'clock and the Fashionable World will have . . . Good gracious, Jacinda! What on earth are you wearing?"

"My lady, whatever can you mean?" Jacinda asked, her wide hazel eyes peeping out from behind a heavy veil of black lace. The veil was attached to a high-crowned black hat that sported no less than three plumes all in the same funereal color as the rest of her ensemble. Even her pelisse was black, with intricate jet beading embroidered on the wide cuffs and high, pointed collar, and her hands were encased in gloves of black kid.

"I mean, missy, that you look all the world as if you're in mourning!" Lady Shipton responded, her lips pursing in annoyance. "I know you possess little fashion sense, but even you must realize that you can't go about dressed like a . . . a crow! Go upstairs and change at once."

Jacinda was grateful for the veil's gossamer protection as she grinned in triumph. She'd found the clothing—last worn to her father's funeral— in the back of her wardrobe, and some imp of mischief had made her don them. The dress was monstrously tight and the pelisse far too heavy for the warm June morning, but the expression on Marchfield's face was well worth the discomfort. Her point made, she rose to her feet with a theatrical sigh.

"Very well, my lady," she said, casting her eyes down demurely. "If that is what you wish, then I shall do as you say. If you will give me but a few minutes, I shall go and change." She started toward the door, only to find her path barred by the duke, who had risen to his feet.

"Pray don't change your clothing on my account, Miss Malvern," he said, his gray eyes piercing the veil to clash with hers. "I find your appearance quite suitable, as I am sure you intended," he added with cool amusement, watching as she stiffened in embarrassment. The moment she had entered the room dressed from head to foot in unrelenting black he knew she had donned the ridiculous clothing in a deliberate attempt to thumb her nose at him. Well, he decided stubbornly, two could play this little game of hers.

"But, Your Grace," the countess protested, exchanging an uneasy look with Cassandra, "I'm sure you must realize I can't allow my niece to go out in society dressed like . . . like this." She indicated Jacinda with a helpless wave of her hand.

"I'm sorry, Lady Shipton, but I'm afraid I must insist," Anthony interrupted, his eyes still fixed on Jacinda's defiant form. "Like you, I have a pressing engagement, and I shall already be shockingly late as it is. If we wait for Miss Mal-

vern to change again, then I fear I'll be forced to postpone our outing until some other day."

"Oh, no, Mama!" Cassandra wailed with disappointment. "You know how much I was counting on this drive! Jacinda looks fine, and besides, why should her appearance matter a whit? She is only there to lend us countenance!"

Lady Shipton was no more eager than her daughter to let such a prime catch as the duke slip through their fingers. And even should he fail to come up to scratch, being seen so constantly in his company could only improve her daughter's consequence. It took her less than a few seconds to reach her decision.

"Very well," she said, raising a hand to rub her throbbing temples. "If Jacinda does not mind looking like a figure from a Cheltenham tragedy, then I'm sure I have no objections. All that I ask is that you have my baby home within the hour. We are attending the ball at the Rochforts' tonight, and she will need to rest if she wishes to be in her best looks."

"I shall do as you ask," Anthony replied, executing a suave bow. "As I shall also be attending the ball, it is in my best interests to see that my favorite dancing partner is well rested. Come along then, Lady Cassandra, Miss Malvern." He favored both ladies with his most devastating smile. "The horses will be growing restless."

Hyde Park was filled with carriages and riders as the duke's black and gold phaeton drawn by a team of perfectly matched blacks turned down Rotten Row. Jacinda had removed the veil from her hat, and surreptitiously unfastened the restrictive buttons on the front of her pelisse, but the gown was still tight enough to hamper her breathing. She was aware of the amused glances being cast in her direction as the phaeton made its way down the green, and she silently cursed the duke's successful ploy. The man was even more clever than she had first suspected, and she was growing annoyed with the easy way he seemed to win their every encounter. Well, she amended, squirming uncomfortably on the squabs, perhaps not *every* encounter. Her eyes took on a reminiscent glow as she remembered his fury when she had tossed the glass of wine in his face. Perhaps she could manage a similar mishap at the Rochforts' ball . . .

Both Marchfield and Cassandra were well known, and progress was slow as they stopped to chat with the crème de la crème of London society. They had just completed their first turn about the park when a rider astride a bay cantered up to join them.

"Marchfield, good to see you again," Lord Jonathan Grayson said, sweeping his curled beaver hat from his head. "And Lady Cassandra, always a delight, I am sure."

"Jonathan." Anthony inclined his head, his eyes resting on the gold fob attached to the younger man's waistcoat. "It has been a long while since last we met. You are well, I trust?"

"Quite well, Marchfield," Lord Jonathan replied, his eyes flickering to Jacinda and Cassandra.

"Hello, Lord Jonathan." Cassandra's greeting was much warmer. She was always willing to have a handsome man pay her court, and gave him a teasing smile. "But why are you out riding in the park? I thought you rakes spent your days at the club gaming away fantastic fortunes?"

"Only those of us who possess such fortunes would dare risk them in so foolish a manner," he replied in a sardonic voice. "We younger sons must behave far more circumspectly, I fear." His dark brown eyes rested on Jacinda, who had remained silent during the brief exchange.

"Miss Malvern," he said with a warm smile. "I'm happy to see you again. I trust you are well?"

"Quite well, sir, I thank you," she said, impressed with his good manners. None of the others had acknowledged her existence beyond a smile. "Were you able to speak to my uncle about Lady Fortune?"

"Not as yet," he replied with apparent indifference. "But I'm sure there's no hurry. My brother seldom retains his interest in anything for very long; I daresay he's forgotten all about it by now."

Lord Jonathan's mount began to dance restlessly, tossing his head in obvious impatience. "I'm afraid I must apologize for Caesar's poor manners," he said, his hands tightening on the reins as he struggled to control the animal. "He hasn't had a good run in a long while, and he is feeling his oats." He touched a finger to his hat. "Ladies, Duke, I shall see you later." And he wheeled the horse around, taking off across the grass at a full gallop.

"I had no idea you were acquainted with Lord

Jonathan's family, Miss Malvern," Anthony said once they resumed their drive. "The new duke is not as socially active as his brother."

"I have never met the duke, Your Grace," Jacinda replied, somewhat surprised by his question. Since they had entered the park he'd barely said two words to her, and she thought he meant to spend the rest of the day gloating.

"But you know his brother, Lord Jonathan?"

"Not really." Jacinda frowned at his persistence. "We've been introduced, of course, but we're really no more than the most casual of acquaintances. He spoke to me a few nights ago about Lady Fortune. His brother apparently wishes to buy her."

"I didn't know Grayson is interested in horses," Anthony replied, hiding his thoughts behind a look of polite interest. He knew Jonathan's brother, if only by reputation, and he was surprised to learn that the elegant dandy would be interested in anything so Corinthian as horseflesh. It probably meant nothing, but in his line of work it was safest not to ignore any possibility. "Well, if such is the case, I must speak with him myself. I have a new Arabian I wish to sell. Quite showy, but not my sort."

"As I told Lord Jonathan, Your Grace, that is something you must discuss with my uncle," Jacinda said, growing bored with the conversation. Horses, she thought in gentle disgust. Was that all men ever thought of?

The earl's carriage was parked in front of the house when Anthony returned with the ladies, and good manners compelled him to escort them inside. He was hoping to wheedle more information from the earl as well, but one look at his ashen face put an end to his schemes.

"Papa, what is it?" Cassandra cried, rushing to her father's side. "What has happened?"

"It's your brother, Wilmount," the earl said wearily, laying a gentle hand on Cassandra's dark curls. "I fear there has been a hunting accident."

"Never say he is d . . . dead!" Cassandra cried, her cheeks paling at the very thought.

"No, I'm sure he's not." The earl sighed, looking troubled. "The message said only that he is badly injured, and that we must come home at once."

While Cassandra dissolved into tears, Jacinda asked, "Where is Aunt Prudence? Has she been told?"

"She's in her room. She took to her bed when I told her." He ran a distracted hand through his thinning hair. "Jacinda, I hate to ask, but could you . . ."

"I'll see to everything," she assured him softly. "I trust you'll want to leave as soon as possible?"

"Yes . . . er . . . that is, I was hoping you could start for Kent without me," he stammered, shooting Anthony a faintly troubled look. "Thing of it is, it's a devilish bad time for me to be away from London. You understand, I am sure, Your Grace. What with Parliament in session, and the prince could need me at any moment . . ."

"Of course, sir, I understand completely," Anthony replied, mulling over this unexpected development. The few papers he had discovered in the earl's desk were worse than useless . . . a diary of some sort containing nothing of import. But it proved Shipton *was* writing. Perhaps the *Journals* were kept in another, safer location—like the earl's study in his country estate. Sir already had a guard on the earl, so his presence was hardly necessary, and with Lady Cassandra away from London he would have no reason to hang about. Thinking quickly, he reached his decision.

"I am very sorry to hear of your son's accident," he said sympathetically. "And I quite understand why you feel you can't abandon your duties here. With your permission, sir, I would be honored to escort your family in your stead."

"That's rare kind of you, Your Grace" the earl said, looking relieved. "I'll own I was at my wits' end wondering what I was to do."

"It will be my pleasure," Anthony assured him with a polite bow. "When should we leave?"

"You must discuss that with Jacinda," Lord Shipton replied in a hearty tone. "The dear child is an ogre of organization. I shall leave it to the two of you to settle the matter between you. Come, Cassandra." He draped a loving arm about the girl's shoulder as he guided her from the room. "I'll take you up to your mama, shall I?"

"Yes, Papa," Cassandra sniffed, dabbing at her dark eyes that still glistened with crystal tears. "And thank you, Your Grace, for lending us your escort. I'm sure Mama and I should have been terrified to have made the journey alone."

"Think nothing of it, Lady Cassandra." He gave the hand she held out to him a brief kiss. "I will see you tomorrow, then."

After they had shut the door behind them,

Jacinda turned to face him. "Will you be able to leave by tomorrow, do you think?" she asked, plans racing through her head as she settled on the gold settee. "If it would be more convenient for you, I suppose we could wait an extra day."

"Tomorrow will be fine," Anthony said, stalking over to stand before her, his silvery-gray eyes resting on her face. "But will that give you adequate time? Packing up a household and removing it to the country takes a great deal of work, you know."

"Indeed I do, sir," Jacinda said, resenting his condescending tone of voice, "but fortunately my uncle has an excellent staff. I'm sure they will prove more than equal to the task. Now if you will excuse me, I must go and talk with our housekeeper. As you say, there is a great deal to be done." She rose, but instead of standing back to allow her to pass, Anthony continued staring down at her.

"What time do you wish to leave? As it is a journey of several hours, we'll have to make an early start of it if we hope to eat at a decent inn," he said, determined to take charge of the matter with or without Miss Malvern's cooperation. His years with Sir had taught him there could be but one commander in any undertaking, and he thought it prudent to establish from the very beginning just who that commander was. "I think we should plan to leave by noon at the latest," he said in a decisive tone.

Jacinda regarded his firmly held jaw and flashing eyes with amusement. When he chose, the duke could be most intimidating. It was a good thing she was not easily cowed, otherwise Marchfield would be impossibly pompous long before they ever reached Kent.

"Two o'clock," she said, her wide smile a feminine version of his own implacability. "That way we can dine here before leaving. Aunt does not travel well on an empty stomach. As to an inn, we shall stop at the Red Hare, I think. Now I really must be going. Good day, Your Grace." And with a final, impudent curtsy, she swept past him, calling out for the butler as she left the room.

Chapter Six

Sir was in his rooms dressing for dinner when Anthony arrived. After apologizing for the interruption he related the afternoon's events to his superior. As he anticipated, Sir found Shipton's reluctance to leave London highly suspect.

"So, he claimed he could not leave the city because of his parliamentary obligations, eh?" he mused, standing before his glass as he added the finishing touches to his cravat. "Rather odd, considering the earl has yet to make it to a single debating session. What else did he say?"

"He alluded to the Privy Council and that the prince might need him at any time," Anthony replied, stepping forward to help Sir into his black silk evening jacket. In keeping with his impoverished image Sir had elected to dispense with the services of a full-time valet, although Anthony thought that was merely an excuse. The other man was notoriously cautious and disliked the notion of allowing anyone becoming too intimate.

"I wonder if the prince is aware of that," Sir remarked, slipping a gold signet ring on his finger. "He can't abide Shipton. The only reason he is on the council at all is because he once loaned the prince some money. Speaking of his lordship, it seems he has had another bit of good fortune."

"Another convenient relative, I take it?"

"Actually"—Sir brushed his dark blond hair back from his forehead with an impatient hand—"this time he's claiming a 'prudent investment.' He's been waving a good deal of blunt around, but whenever he's pressed for details, he turns as coy as a Bath miss. I'm checking into it."

"Perhaps I should stay," Anthony said with a worried frown. "I'll escort the ladies down as I promised, and then come—"

"No," Sir interrupted, flicking the lace of his cuffs back and sliding a wicked-looking stiletto up his sleeve. "We'll keep an eye on the earl for you. The most important thing is that you gain entry to the house so that you can search it thoroughly. If you don't find the *Journals* in his study, keep looking. I'd try the library; neither his wife nor his daughter strikes me as being very literary, and it would make an excellent hiding place."

"Very good, Sir," Anthony replied. Although it was unlikely the countess or Lady Cassandra would venture into the library, the same could not be said of Miss Malvern. He would have to take special pains to avoid tripping over her. "Anything else?"

"When you find the *Journals,* send word through the usual channels, and he'll be detained. Remember, the *Journals* are the key, and it is vital that they be located. At all cost," he added, his blue eyes meeting Anthony's in the mirror.

"As you say, Sir." Anthony understood at once. "I'll do everything within my power."

"I know you will, Marchfield, I trust you implicitly. By the by"—he turned to pick up his evening cane and gloves—"I'll be incommunicado for the next few weeks. If you encounter any difficulty in Folkstone, you are to go directly to the navy yard at Dover. They have orders to give you whatever assistance you require."

Something in Sir's tone made Anthony uneasy, and he studied his face with mounting concern. "Is there anything wrong, Sir?"

"We lost another two agents," he said without preamble. "And I have reason to believe there will be an attempt on my life as well."

"My God!" Anthony gasped, paling at Sir's blunt words. "What are you going to do?"

"Go into hiding and see who comes looking," he replied in a pragmatic manner. "I've taken care that only a few people will know my exact whereabouts. If the killer finds me, I'll know precisely who the traitor is."

Anthony uttered a blistering curse beneath his breath. Violent death was a risk every man accepted when he joined the organization, but that death should come as a result of betrayal seemed doubly obscene. He drew a steadying breath, his hands balling into tight fists. "What are their names?" he asked in a dangerously soft voice.

Sir smiled slightly. "I'm afraid I can't tell you, Anthony. I trust you with my honor and my life, but the less you know about this, the better." He paused as if searching for the right words, then said, "If I fail, I've left word with the prince that you are to take command. Your first duty will be to eliminate the two men I suspect. All the information is in a letter to be opened after my death. Question them if you can do so safely, but if not . . ." His shrug was eloquent.

"But, Sir, if you're in danger, why don't you arrest them now?" Anthony protested in alarm. "Give me their names, and I'll get you whatever information you want, I promise you!"

"I'm sure you would," Sir murmured wryly. "But that's not the answer. Rest assured that they've been isolated so they can't cause any more harm."

"But—"

"The important thing is that we learn everything they have said, and to whom they have said it," Sir said sternly. "If we act prematurely and arrest the spy, we eliminate only the most visible part of the problem. I want the leader, and I mean to have him. Even if it means my life. Agreed?"

"Agreed," Anthony answered quietly, knowing he had no other choice. Sir was right, of course. The safety of the country outweighed the life of any single man.

"Good." Sir gave him a reassuring smile. "Now

if you will excuse me, I have a rather pressing dinner engagement."

"Anyone I know?" he asked in a determined attempt to change the subject.

Sir's smile deepened. "Madame Bouchett. It seems she has developed a taste for variety, and now that Shipton is distracted by family responsibilities, she finds herself at loose ends." He turned back to the mirror, giving his cravat a finishing tug. "Farewell, Anthony. Duty calls."

Anthony arrived at Berkeley Square shortly before noon, hoping for an early start. But if he thought to coerce Jacinda with such methods, she was quick to disabuse him of the notion. After relieving him of his hat and greatcoat, she simply escorted him into the parlor and told him to wait until her aunt and cousin joined him.

"And when will that be?" he demanded, studying her with marked suspicion. Despite the brevity of their association, he felt he knew her fairly well. She might look as innocent as a nun's hen, but he knew that beneath her prim gray gown and demure chignon there lurked a hellcat. What amazed him most was that he was becoming rather fond of that hellcat.

"Oh, not long. An hour, perhaps two," Jacinda replied, surveying the duke from beneath her thick lashes. In his traveling coat of hunter-green serge and his buckskin breeches he looked quite handsome. Cassie would doubtlessly swoon with delight when she saw him.

"Two?" Anthony's brows lowered in an angry scowl. "But I wanted to leave early!"

"As did I, Your Grace," came the placid reply. "But unfortunately my aunt and cousin decided to sleep in this morning so that they would be well rested for the journey. They have only just risen, and I fear it will be some time before they'll be ready to leave. However, I'll send them word that you have arrived and are waiting for them. Perhaps that will sway them." She infused just enough doubt in her voice to let him know she considered this most unlikely.

"Thank you, Miss Malvern," he said, a muscle flexing in his cheek. Logically, he knew she wasn't to blame for the delay, but he was still hard-pressed not to hold her responsible. It was those eyes of hers, he decided broodingly, that green and gold dance of light in the hazel that made it obvious she was enjoying a secret laugh at him.

"You're most welcome, Sir," Jacinda answered, wondering if she should dare risk a curtsy. The duke appeared at the end of his tether, and she suspected it would take little to make him lose his formidable temper. Then she remembered she would have to travel in his company for the next several hours, and decided to be prudent. It made for an interesting change.

"If you desire anything, you have only to ring for the footman," she said, giving him the smile she usually reserved for sulky children and recalcitrant tradesmen. "Now if you will excuse me, I must return to the packing."

"Wait." His fingers closed around her arm as she turned to go.

"Yes, Your Grace?" She gave him a quizzical look.

Anthony felt a faint flush of color touch his cheeks. He had no idea why he had stopped her; he only knew that he didn't want her to leave just yet. Stalling, he said, "I was wondering if your uncle might be here. I wanted to assure him I would take every care in escorting his lovely family to Kent. I wouldn't want him to worry."

"He has already left," she answered guardedly, wondering what was going on behind that dazzling smile. He used it whenever he wanted something, she realized, or when he was being particularly evasive. That reminded her of yesterday, and the fact that he still hadn't explained himself to her. She tilted her head to one side, giving him her most innocent look.

"I'm sure you needn't worry about that, Your Grace. My uncle trusts you completely. He didn't even seem to mind the fact that you were in his study."

Anthony's fingers dug into Jacinda's arms. "You told him that?" he demanded roughly, pulling her against him with unconscious force. "What did he say?"

Jacinda winced with pain. She hadn't expected so strong a reaction, and fought to free herself from his bruising hold. "Unhand me, sir!" she snapped, glaring up into his face. "How dare you treat me so!"

Anthony loosened his fingers at once, already regretting his impetuous action. If she wasn't suspicious of him before this, she undoubtedly was now. He stepped back from her, his eyes never leaving her face as he said, "I apologize for my behavior, Miss Malvern. I meant you no insult, I assure you. But I cannot tolerate you spreading tales behind my back. I must know what you told the earl."

Jacinda's jaw dropped at such brass. "Spreading tales!" she cried. "You opened my uncle's desk, and you were reading his personal papers! I would hardly consider *that* the actions of an innocent man, and—"

"Is that what you told your uncle?"

"No, but I want an explanation, and don't think you can get around me like you did yesterday, because I won't allow—"

"What did you tell your uncle?"

Jacinda tossed her hands in the air in exasperation. "Nothing!" she shouted angrily. "I told him nothing! How could I? I spent half the night packing, and the other half tending to my aunt. But I mean to tell him, the very next time I see him! And then, Your Grace, you may explain yourself to him."

"You won't tell him." He said the words with such smug confidence that Jacinda felt like boxing his ears.

"Oh, won't I?" she taunted. "And pray, sir, why is that?"

"Because," Anthony said complacently, "I'll deny it. Who do you think he'll believe, Jacinda? You, or a potential son-in-law?"

She flushed in outrage, too angry to note he had used her Christian name. He was right. If it came down to believing her or the very rich, very eligible Duke of Marchfield, her uncle would unhesitatingly side with the duke. He would be furious with her, so furious he might even order her from his house. Until she could provide for herself, she dared not risk it. She knew it, and judging from his self-satisfied smirk, so did the duke.

"Very good, Your Grace," she said, drawing herself up as she met his gaze. "Round one to you. But I shall be watching you. You're up to something, and one day I shall prove it!" And with that she stormed from the room.

In the end, it was well after one before they were able to leave London. Jacinda, the duke, and the Creighton ladies traveled in his crested coach, while the servants went ahead with the baggage. Jacinda sat quietly in her corner, listening to the others gossip as she gazed out at the passing scenery with troubled eyes.

The more she thought of what had passed between her and the duke, the more puzzled she became. Despite the evidence to the contrary she was certain he was innocent of any wrongdoing. He was far too proud for one thing, and her instincts told her he was a man of impeccable honor. Yet why had he reacted as he had? And what had he been doing searching in her uncle's desk? None of it made any sense.

Sitting across from her, Anthony was aware of Jacinda's confusion as well as the furtive glances she cast him when she thought he wasn't looking. He wanted to reassure her, but there was no way he could do so without jeopardizing his mission. He didn't know why, but it was important to him that Miss Malvern think well of him. With the exception of Sir, he'd never given a fig what the world thought of him. But with her it was different, and that troubled him. The mission before him was difficult and dangerous, and he couldn't allow personal considerations to distract him. Regardless, he had to do his duty.

The journey to Folkstone passed quickly, with stops at Maidstone and Charing. With his usual foresight the duke had his valet travel ahead, and there were always fresh horses and warm food awaiting them at each inn where they stopped. Less than five hours after leaving London they reached Shipton Hall.

The manor house was located on a cliff less than a mile out of the town. The front of the house faced the park with rose-colored bricks and mullioned windows and the back was to the sea. Anthony barely had time to study the house's tactical position before the carriage rumbled to a halt, and the countess and Lady Cassandra leapt out and dashed inside.

Jacinda flicked the duke a nervous glance. In the ordinary scheme of things her aunt should have been the one to escort their noble guest inside and see him comfortably settled, but now apparently the task had fallen to her. "You must forgive my aunt, Your Grace," she began hesitantly. "But she has been quite concerned about Wilmount." This was the first time they had been alone since the scene in the parlor, and she was uncertain how she should behave.

"I know," Anthony replied in a gentle voice, hoping to set her at her ease. "And I quite understand her wishing to rush to his side." He gestured toward the footman who was still holding the door for them. "Shall we join the others?"

"Oh." She colored in embarrassment. "Of course, Your Grace. If you'll kindly follow me, I will have you shown to your room."

After escorting the duke inside, Jacinda excused herself and then went off to confer with the housekeeper. As she had expected, Willie had been shaken in his fall, but not badly injured. One of his friends, who was almost as much of a dolt as Wilmount, fired off the note, claiming the viscount was all but at death's door. Satisfied with what Mrs. McGivvey had told her, she arranged for a light dinner to be served within the hour, and then went off to check on her cousin.

She found Wilmount in his room, propped up on a nest of pillows, surrounded by his anxious mother and sister.

"Hello, Willie," she said, greeting her elder cousin with a smile. "I hear your pride took a tumble."

"My pride, indeed!" Wilmount Cedric Creighton, Viscount Shipton, scoffed in a thin voice, his brown eyes flashing in indignation. "That great brute of a horse threw me into a hedge and then tried to trample me! Dr. Haverlock said it was a miracle I wasn't killed. As it is, I have been told I must have complete rest if I am ever to recover."

"I see." Jacinda's lips twitched in amusement. "Well, in that case I am happy to see you doing so well." Her eyes went to the countess, who was grasping her son's hand and gazing down into his flushed face as if she expected his imminent demise.

"I've given the duke the Royal Suite, Aunt," she said in her most pragmatic manner. "I've also arranged for a light dinner to be served at the usual hour. Shall you be dining with us, or would you prefer to take your meal here?"

"I'll eat with my baby," the countess declared, brushing a strand of brown hair back from Wilmount's forehead. "Cassandra may act as hostess in my stead."

"Yes, Mama," Cassie answered, obviously pleased with the news. Now that she had reassured herself as to her brother's health, she was anxious to get out of her dusty clothing. She pressed a quick kiss on his cheek and then hurried from the room.

Jacinda spent another fifteen minutes listening to Wilmount's litany of suffering before excusing herself on the pretext that she had to see to the guests' comfort. In addition to the duke there were also three of the viscount's friends in residence, all of whom were thankfully out riding at the moment. She was on her way back down to the kitchens to chat with the cook, when she encountered Anthony, who had just stepped out of his room.

"Hello again, Miss Malvern," he said, giving her a cautious smile. Even though he had changed she was still in her traveling clothes, and he wondered if she had even had a moment to rest since their arrival. "How is the viscount?" he asked, falling into step beside her as they walked down the carpeted hall. "I was going to visit him, but I thought it might be best to wait."

"He's fine," she said, remembering the childish

pout on Willie's face as she left his room. "And I'm certain he would welcome the company."

Anthony was enchanted by the dimple that appeared beside her mouth. Her hair had worked its way free from her bun to curl about her cheeks, and his fingers itched with the sudden desire to brush it back. The impulse left him feeling faintly shocked, and he resolutely put the thought from his mind.

"Then I'll visit him after dinner," he said, hiding his confusion behind a cool facade. "Also, my valet informs me that there are several other guests as well. Do you happen to know their names? Perhaps I am acquainted with them."

"There is a Mr. Peter Blakely, a Mr. Daniel Vale, and the Marquess of Aimsford. Are you acquainted with him, sir?"

"I know of him," Anthony answered slowly, his heart beginning to race with excitement. "Is he a very good friend of your cousin's? That is," he added at her suspicious scowl, "the marquess is somewhat of a high stickler. Not at all the sort to go racketing about with a young rakehell like the viscount."

Jacinda grinned at the thought of her priggish cousin being called "a rakehell." "Well, to be honest, his lordship is more my uncle's friend than he is Willie's," she confided with a laugh. "They spend hours closeted away in his study working on bloodlines. The marquess is quite a horseman, you know."

"Indeed I do." Anthony kept his voice carefully neutral. Finally, he thought, a direct link between the earl and a French agent. They had been after the marquess for months now, but he'd always managed to stay one step ahead of them. If they could tie him to Lady X . . . His eyes gleamed at the prospect.

They parted company at the bottom of the wide staircase, and while Jacinda went off to attend to her duties, Anthony conducted a brief reconnaissance of the house. In addition to the bedchambers, parlors, and drawing rooms, there was also a library, ballroom, and dining room in the main wing. The west wing contained several guest suites as well as a billiards room and game room that was well stocked with rifles and a brace of dueling pistols. He was standing in front of the case admiring the weapons when the sound of masculine laughter reached his ears. He turned just as the door burst open and three men came hurrying in.

"Ah, reinforcements at last!" The first man, a young dandy with bright red hair and an equally bright yellow hunting jacket, advanced toward Anthony, his hand outstretched in greeting. "We are so heartily sick of one another's company that we are ready to commit murder! I am Peter Blakely."

"I am Anthony Selton, Duke of Marchfield," Anthony answered, accepting the man's hand. His gray eyes swept over the younger man, taking in his open, friendly face and guileless blue eyes before dismissing him as harmless. He turned to the second man, who was hovering uncertainly by the map table. "Mr. Vale, I take it?"

"D . . . Daniel Vale, sir . . . Your Grace," he stammered, his plump cheeks reddening with a telling blush. "Happy to make your acquaintance, Your Grace."

"Mr. Vale," Anthony said, his attention shifting to the dark-haired man standing beside the suit of armor in the far corner. "Lord Aimsford," he acknowledged with a stiff bow. "This is a pleasant surprise."

"Is it?" Richard Dryden, the Marquess of Aimsford, drawled in his most affected tones, studying Anthony down the length of his long nose. He was an almost cadaverously thin man, with skin as white as a girl's and piercing black eyes. He wore his thinning dark hair in an unfashionable queue, and his blue coat with gilded buttons and baggy cream breeches were equally unstylish. He looked for all the world like a dancing master down on his luck, but Anthony knew better than to underestimate his intellect.

"Enough of this, where are the ladies?" Peter demanded, his eyes bright with excitement. "Willie promised us there would be ladies!"

"Lady Shipton and Lady Cassandra are with the viscount," Anthony replied, flashing the young dandy an encouraging smile. "But I'm sure they'll be joining us for dinner."

"Only two? How disappointing," he sighed, his face almost comically downcast. "Whatever will the three of you do for feminine companionship?"

"Is . . . is Miss Jacinda not with the ladies?" Mr. Vale inquired anxiously, his pale blue eyes flicking in Anthony's direction. "I . . . I was certain she would be here."

Was the young cub actually interested in that

she-devil, Anthony wondered, feeling faintly disturbed by the notion. "Miss Malvern is with the cook at the moment," he informed Mr. Vale in a cool tone. "But I'm sure she will be joining us as soon as she is finished."

"Well, I suppose I shouldn't hog all the ladies," Peter said with a laugh. "You are welcome to Miss Jacinda, Daniel, although I wish you joy of her. She really is the most bookish creature, with scarcely a word to say for herself. Can't think of what the two of you have to talk about."

"She likes S . . . Shakespeare and Milton, we talk of them and about writing."

"May the good lord above preserve me from literary-minded ladies." Peter sniffed, affecting a delicate yawn. "Next you will say that *you* are writing a book."

"I am," Daniel admitted, ducking his head shyly. "Miss Jacinda is helping me."

"Quelle horreur," Peter said with a shudder. "It is not to be borne! Don't you agree, Aimsford? The last thing our society needs is another scribbler. First we have Byron's weary cantos and then those malicious journals by Lady X! What next, I ask you?"

"Am I to take it you don't like the *Journals*, Mr. Blakely?" Anthony asked, his hooded eyes searching the marquess's thin face for any betraying sign of emotion. "They are generally held to be quite popular."

"I rest my case." Peter tossed his head. "A thing, especially a literary work, cannot be both good *and* popular. The two terms are mutually exclusive. Besides, the dreadful creature has yet to include me in a single book! I hate being snubbed."

Despite himself, Anthony's lips twitched in amusement. "I'm sure it's only an oversight on the author's part," he said, still keeping a sharp eye on Aimsford. "If she knew you, I daresay she would be unable to resist using you."

"That's true," Peter agreed, looking smug. "I am eminently worthy of satirizing. I shall have to write the publisher a note and tell him so."

"I know Lady X."

"What?" The roar of disbelief all but drowned out Mr. Vale's shy pronouncement, as the other three men turned to gape at him.

"You do not!" Peter exclaimed, shooting his friend a disdainful look. "You don't know anybody."

"You really mustn't say such things, Mr. Vale." The marquess's aquiline nose twitched in disapproval. "Falsehoods once uttered are not easily recalled."

Mr. Vale's brows lowered and his bottom lip thrust forward. "I *do* know her," he insisted in a petulant voice. "And so do you."

"What do you mean, Mr. Vale?" Anthony asked with growing alarm. Secrecy was vital if the mission was to succeed, and such talk was decidedly dangerous. "I'm sure you must be mistaken," he added in his most dampening tones, hoping to discourage the younger man from pursuing his claim. But instead of intimidating him, his words only seemed to make Mr. Vale that much more determined.

"I tell you that I *do* know her," he insisted indignantly. "Well, not her name perhaps, but I do know her, and it's obvious she knows me . . . and you too, Lord Aimsford," he added, looking childishly pleased at being the center of so much attention.

"Explain that, sir!" the marquess demanded, his thin lips pursing with disapproval. "I am certain I have never met this creature in my life!"

"It was here, last summer," Mr. Vale continued in his dogmatic way. "You remember, my lord. We were all down here for a hunt, and I was telling you all about my brother's adventures on the peninsula, and you told us about the smugglers hereabouts. Do you recall the conversation?"

"Vaguely," the marquess admitted, "but I don't see what that has to do with Lady X, or your ridiculous insistence that I somehow know her!"

"But don't you see? It was there, our very conversation set down word for word in the last journal! I read it myself, and there's more!"

"More?"

"There were at least two other conversations we had that weekend set down in the journal, and a fairly accurate account of Lady Cassandra's hunting accident. Don't you see?" he repeated, gesticulating wildly. "Lady X is not Byron or Hazlitt, or anyone else! She's one of us; and she's here in this very house!"

Chapter Seven

There was a moment of stunned silence, and then everyone began talking at once. "Good gad, Daniel! Are you quite certain about all of this?" Peter's voice rose above the cacophony.

"Dead certain," Mr. Vale answered. "It was all there in the *Journals;* even that unfortunate remark Richard made about the Duke of York."

"Well, I'll be damned." Peter collapsed on the nearest chair, staring at Daniel with wide eyes. "I do believe you're right. The question is, what are we going to do about it?"

"Nothing." Anthony spoke firmly, determined to put an end to the dangerous speculation. "The matter is none of our concern, and I suggest we leave well enough alone."

"None of our concern!" Aimsford's chest swelled with indignation. "That's easy enough for you to say, Your Grace. *You've* never been the victim of this . . . this viper's poisonous tongue!"

"Perhaps not," Anthony agreed warily, intrigued by the marquess's vehemence. If Lord Shipton was Lady X, then it was obvious Aimsford knew nothing of it, which opened a whole new line of speculation. "But I don't see why you're so anxious to uncover this Lady X. What possible good would it do?"

"Really, Marchfield, how can you be such a slow top?" Peter complained with a pout. "Lady X has been the talk of London for the past two seasons. If we succeed in unmasking her, our place in society will be assured."

"Nevertheless, I don't think we should involve ourselves in something that—"

"You may relax, sir, for you aren't being asked to involve yourself in anything," Peter assured him with a haughty glare. "This is *our* mystery, and we shall be the ones to solve it. Now"—he turned eagerly to the others—"what should be our first course of action?"

"Well," Mr. Vale said, scratching his ear thoughtfully, "I suppose we should draw up the names of everyone who was present that weekend, and then invite them back down. With Willie's permission, of course."

"Daniel, you are brilliant!" Peter enthused, clapping his hands. "My apologies for all those times I called you a mutton brain. Yes, we shall assemble all our suspects under one roof and then . . . then what?"

"Demand that the scoundrel confess, of course!" the marquess growled, slapping his thigh with his riding quirt.

"And naturally she will agree." Peter gave him a disdainful look. "Use your head, sir! If Lady X has eluded detection this long, what makes you think she will confess all in a grand denouncement? Besides, what fun would that be? No, we must trap her first."

"How?"

"Well, how should I know? Really, Daniel, must I think of everything?" Peter gave a dramatic sigh. "All of this mental activity has given me the headache, and I must rest if I am to be at all presentable for dinner. Let's plan to meet in the study before the ladies join us, and we'll go over our plans then." He flicked a somber-faced Anthony a teasing smirk. "All except you, of course, Marchfield. I understand perfectly why you don't wish to help us. So sordid, you know."

"I didn't say I wouldn't help you," Anthony began, a desperate plan forming in his mind. If he was unable to prevent the others from seeking out Lady X, then at the very least he could hope to lead them far from their quarry.

"Oh, no, we wouldn't think of involving you against your will," Peter assured him with a brilliant smile. "A halfhearted conspirator is of no use at all. Only look at the problems that tiresome Brutus caused with all of his shilly-shallying. If *you* wish to seek out Lady X, then you may certainly do so with our blessings. In fact, I think you should. A thousand pounds says we shall be the ones to find her first! What say you now, Marchfield?"

Never in his worst nightmares had Anthony thought his carefully conceived plans could go so terribly awry. Secrecy was essential to the success of the mission, and a wager such as this was bound to cause a scandal. He dreaded to think what Sir would make of this when he heard the news.

"I say, Peter, that doesn't seem very sporting to me." Mr. Vale spoke first, his brow knitting in concern. "Three against one hardly seems fair."

"You're right," Peter admitted, laying a finger to his lips as he considered the matter. Then he gave a sudden exclamation. "I have it! Instead of the three of us working together against the duke, we shall all operate on our own, and the first person to learn Lady X's identity wins the thousand pounds!" He surveyed the others with a delighted grin. "Well, what say you, gentlemen? Is it a bet?"

After leaving the game room Anthony went up to his rooms and changed into his riding clothes. The afternoon's debacle left him feeling trapped, and he hoped a brisk ride across the countryside would help blow the cobwebs from his head. Apparently he wasn't the only person seeking solace in the fresh air; Miss Malvern was already in the stable yard and ready to leave when he arrived.

"Good afternoon, sir!" she called out to him from the back of a bay mare. "Would you care to join me in a ride?"

Anthony gazed up at her, admiring the picture she made in her riding habit of bottle-green tarlatan, her hair tucked beneath her beaver hat. The solitude he had been seeking a few minutes earlier now seemed unimportant, and he gave her a warm smile.

"A ride sounds just the thing, Miss Malvern," he said, walking over to stand before her mount. He ran a gloved hand down the bay's flanks, pleased by the horse's delicate symmetry. If the other horses in the earl's stable were like this one, then he wouldn't bother sending for his own hunter.

As if reading his mind, Jacinda said, "I know Uncle would want you to make use of his stables, Your Grace. He has a black stallion, Nightwind, he's very proud of. Perhaps you would care to give him a try?"

"The colt out of Sedrian?" Anthony brightened at the news. "I'd forgotten your uncle purchased him at Tatts. If you'll give me a moment, Miss Malvern, I'll mount up and join you."

Jacinda waited while he disappeared into the stables, controlling her horse's restive movements with an agile flick of her wrist. Lady Jane was one of her favorite mounts, but she was a trifle spirited and she knew she would have to look sharp if she hoped to keep her seat.

"I hope you will live up to your name and be a lady," she told the horse, patting its neck with her free hand. "If you misbehave and throw me in front of the duke, I'm not sure I shall ever forgive you."

Anthony rejoined her a short time later, astride a coal-black stallion. He was dressed in a claret riding jacket with cream-colored breeches, and Jacinda had to admit he was quite handsome. When he caught her studying him and gave her a quizzical look, she said, "If you want to ride ahead, Your Grace, please don't wait on my account. Nightwind likes a good run."

"I'm sure he does," Anthony replied, his large hands easily holding the animal in check. "But this time he will have to play the gentleman." He touched his whip to his hat in salute. "Shall we go, Miss Malvern? After that long carriage ride, I could use a bit of fresh air."

They rode east across the fields, heading toward the cliffs. They paused on the edge, and

Anthony settled back in his saddle as he enjoyed
the breathtaking beauty of the scene below him.

"You're fortunate to have such natural beauty
around you, Miss Malvern. If I had such a view
on my doorstep, I'm not sure I would ever venture from home."

Jacinda smiled in pleasure, watching the gray
and white waves crashing against the black rocks
and sending their salt-laden spray into the air. "I
do love the sea," she confessed with a sigh. "It's
wild and unpredictable, and it will never be fully
mastered. If I were a man, I think I'd join the
navy and sail off to the very ends of the earth."

"A most romantic notion," he said, tearing his
eyes from the restless waves to study the dreamy
expression on her face. "However, I fear life
aboard ship is not as pleasant as one may think.
It's filled with hard work and danger, and that
wild sea you so admire can turn killer with a shift
of the wind. But"—his lips quirked suddenly—
"I quite agree with you. If given the chance, I'd
have given anything to have gone into the navy."

Jacinda stared at him in surprise. "But you're a
man," she said, obviously confused. "You're not
bound by such ridiculous conventions as we
women must endure! You're free to do whatever
you want."

"I'm also a duke, the last of my line," Anthony
said, his lips twisting with bitter memory. "And
it was decided that my first duty was to survive
long enough to perpetuate the Selton line. When
I tried purchasing a commission, my father had
the king stop me."

"How?" Jacinda was frankly curious.

"By ordering me home," he answered, reliving again the humiliation he had felt when the old king had torn up his papers. He had never forgiven his father for his interference, and after his death he tried enlisting again. His request was refused, but this time he was contacted by Sir, who offered him a unique way of serving his country and his king.

Realizing he had been silent for several minutes and that Miss Malvern was casting him worried glances, Anthony touched his spurs to Nightwind's flanks, making the animal dance nervously. "It would appear my horse doesn't share our aesthetic appreciation of the sea, Miss Malvern," he said, his hands tightening on the reins. "Perhaps I should give him his head. Will you be all right by yourself?"

"Of course, Your Grace," Jacinda answered placidly. She had seen him make surreptitious use of his spurs, and knew he doubtlessly wanted to be alone. "Lady Jane and I know how to find our way home, don't we, girl?"

"Very well, if you're certain, I'll leave you two ladies to your own devices." He wheeled the horse around and took off at a full gallop, trying to outrun the troubling specters of the past and present that pursued him.

"Jacinda, I should like a word with you, if you don't mind." Lady Shipton waylaid Jacinda as she stepped out into the hallway.

"Of course, Aunt Prudence, what is it?" Jacinda asked, gazing at her aunt politely. She was dressed for dinner in her favorite gown of gold muslin trimmed with darker gold lace, her light brown hair tumbling to her shoulders in gentle waves. The gown was much grander than her usual style, and she convinced herself that she wore it in honor of their first dinner home. Certainly the duke's presence at the table had nothing to do with her decision.

"Not out here," the countess said, glancing around her nervously. "Come inside." And she dragged Jacinda into the sitting room.

"Is something wrong, ma'am?" Jacinda queried, puzzled by her aunt's actions. "There's nothing wrong with Wilmount, is there?" She seized upon the most likely explanation for her aunt's behavior.

"Oh, no, he's fine, or rather he's as fine as might be expected considering he was almost killed," Lady Shipton said, distracted by the mention of her beloved son. "He's far too delicate to be riding those dangerous beasts, and so I told him. But he will persist on riding them to please his father even though he is terrified of them, poor lamb. But that's not why I brought you in here."

"Then what is the reason?" Jacinda prodded, anxious to join the others in the parlor. Because of their late arrival dinner was almost two hours behind schedule, and she wanted to make her apologies to the guests in person. Lord knew they had to be half-starved by now.

"Wilmount has decided he wants a house party," Lady Shipton said, wringing her hands nervously. "He has a list of people he wants invited down, and he insists they be sent for at once. I tried explaining that as the season is not yet officially ended we really should wait, but he grew so agitated, I told him I would see to it." She bit her lip, blinking back tears. "You don't think his fall affected his brain, do you?"

It took all of her willpower, but Jacinda managed not to break into laughter. Trust her aunt to come up with so ridiculous a notion, she thought, schooling her features to show nothing but polite concern. "Of course I don't, Aunt," she soothed, laying a comforting hand on her arm. "I'm sure Willie is fine; he is probably just hungry for company, that's all."

"Well, how can we be sure?" her aunt argued worriedly. "He wouldn't be the first man turned into an idiot by an accidental blow on the head. Look at Lord Fennington. He was bright as could be until he fell off the roof; now he wanders about in sheets pretending to be Julius Caesar!"

"If Willie takes to wearing the bedclothes and spouting Latin, we can worry then," Jacinda said decisively. "In the meanwhile, why don't you give me the guest list and I'll send off the invitations for you."

"Will you?" Her aunt's blinding smile told her she had played right in the countess's hands. "Bless you, my dear, I am sure." She dug the list out of her pocket and thrust it at Jacinda. "Now you're certain this won't interfere with your other duties?" she asked with such false solicitude that Jacinda almost lost her composure.

"I'm quite sure, Aunt," she said, thinking that it had been well over a week since she had last touched the *Journals.* She'd have to work twice as hard to get the manuscript to her publisher on the agreed-upon date. "He'll also be wanting a ball and the usual entertainments, I presume?"

"Of course." Lady Shipton was now all smiles. "But I shall leave that up to your discretion. I'm sure you'll do an excellent job, you always do." She gave Jacinda's cheek a condescending pat. "Now we must hurry to join our guests; it's bad form to keep them waiting, you know."

Jacinda spent the next week managing the estate and doing what writing she could. Her familial duties occupied the greater part of her afternoons, leaving only the evenings free for her writing. This meant she saw little of the duke and the others, a situation which was not at all to her liking. She tried telling herself that this was the price she must pay for her craft, but she still felt consumed with resentment, especially on those evenings when she saw Cassie and Marchfield laughing over a hand of faro.

It didn't help that the writing wasn't going as well as she expected. For one thing the character of Lord Stiffback, once so promising, had deteriorated into something dangerously resembling the hero of one of Mrs. Radcliffe's gothics.

Even the journal itself had changed, and rather than being a biting satire of a vain and frivolous society, it was now a lighthearted, tongue-in-cheek portrayal of the upper class. It had sparkle and life, and she admitted the writing was some of the best she had done, but it lacked Lady X's astringent humor. After spending two evenings in a row attempting to get the book back to its original concept, she admitted defeat and started rewriting the manuscript from scratch, hoping her publisher would not be disagreeably surprised by her new style.

A few days after she'd sent off the last of the invitations, Shipton Hall was invaded by guests. Aunt Prudence seemed greatly surprised by the quick response, although Jacinda was less innocent. Three of the invited guests were matchmaking mamas with their nubile daughters in tow. With the duke and the other highly eligible bachelors present, she would hardly have expected otherwise.

The earl returned with the flood of visitors, bringing Lord Jonathan Grayson with him. The younger man had come to look over the earl's horseflesh, and he apologized politely to Jacinda at having arrived unannounced.

"Not at all, sir," she said, flashing him a grateful smile. She thought it very astute of him to recognize that although Lady Shipton was nominally his hostess, it was she who would be doing the majority of the work. "Another eligible bachelor is always welcome at house parties, I promise you."

"You forget I am but a younger son," he said, bowing over her hand, his brown eyes noting every aspect of her prim blue gown and coronet of braids. "I fear some of the ladies present, especially Lady Shipton and Lady Carlisle, may think me less than 'eligible.'"

"Nonsense," she replied briskly, feeling a faint twinge of pity that he had noticed the countess's and marchioness's gentle snubbing. She knew what it was like to be shoved aside, and she made a vow to be sure he was included in all the outings she had planned. It would mean she would have to come up with another lady to even out their numbers, but she was sure this wouldn't be a great problem. There were enough gently bred girls in the neighborhood who would like nothing better than to be included.

That night she decided to forgo writing and join the others. Settling the skirts of her white and green gown about her, she set out to make herself pleasant to their guests. The first person she sought out was Mr. Vale, who was sitting by himself in the far corner of the salon.

"You are looking rather pensive, Mr. Vale," she teased, her hazel eyes meeting his. "Is something troubling you?" She raised a glass of sherry to her lips as she asked the question.

"Actually," Mr. Vale confessed, turning eagerly toward her, "I was wondering which of these folk might be Lady X."

Jacinda began choking, tears streaming down her cheeks as she struggled for breath. "What did you say?" she wheezed.

"I said, I was wondering which of these folk might be Lady X," Mr. Vale repeated, his eyes worried as they took in her flushed face and overly bright eyes. "I say, Miss Jacinda, are you quite sure you're feeling the thing? Perhaps you would like some more sherry." He made as if to rise.

"No!" She grabbed his arm, staying him. "No, Mr. Vale, I'm fine, I assure you. I . . . I . . .

whatever makes you think that Lady X might be here in this room?"

He repeated his story of the house party last summer, adding that he was more convinced than ever that Lady X had to be one of their circle. "For she seems to know everyone," he concluded, looking pleased with his deductive powers. "And you must own 'tis strange that she repeated Richard's conversation word for word. You remember it, Miss Jacinda; you were there after all."

"Er . . . yes, so I was," she agreed, silently cursing her decision to use the delicious *on-dit* of the duke falling off his horse while reviewing the troops. She usually avoided using anything that might be directly traced to her, but Richard Vale's droll comment that the duke was merely inspecting the shine on his men's boots had been irresistible. She wished now that she'd resisted a trifle harder.

"But, Mr. Vale, that still doesn't prove that Lady X is . . . er . . . one of us," she continued lamely, her mind whirling as she sought some way out of this contretemps. "That story made all the rounds in London. Why, anybody could be Lady X!"

"But Richard's remark wasn't repeated," Mr. Vale insisted in his earnest fashion. "And what about that fall Lady Cassandra took while we were hunting? I know none of us breathed a word of it, so who else could it have been?"

Again Jacinda cursed the malicious streak in her that had compelled her to include Cassie's tumble in the last book. If Cassie hadn't whipped her little mount afterward, insisting the poor

creature be destroyed, she would never have
done so reckless a thing. But she had been so
angry . . .

"You still don't have any proof," she main-
tained firmly, hoping to convince Mr. Vale of his
folly. "And besides, so what if one of our guests
is Lady X. It's really none of your concern, you
know."

He gave her a startled look. "That's what
Marchfield said."

"The duke knows of this . . . this theory of
yours?" Jacinda gasped, paling in horror.

"Everyone knows," came the reply. "That is,
Peter, Lord Aimsford, the duke, and Willie, of
course. We have a bet, you see, and the first person to unmask Lady X wins a thousand pounds.
That's why we invited everyone back here. It was
my idea," he added, looking to her for approval.

She glanced about the room, realizing to her
horror that he was right. With the exception of
the duke and Lord Jonathan, the elegant assem-
blage of persons in the Shipton salon was the
same as it had been last summer. She closed her
eyes, fighting off the desire to swoon. This was
her worst fear come to life, and she was power-
less to do anything about it.

Anthony stepped out into the garden from the
salon, closing the door quietly behind him. Most
of the company had already retired, and those
who remained awake were deeply involved in a
game of faro. If he was going to make a try for
the *Journals,* it would have to be tonight. With the
hunt for Lady X well under way he couldn't risk

the possibility one of the others would tumble on to the truth.

Not that there was much chance of that, he thought, extracting a cheroot from his pocket case and placing it between his lips, for a bigger collection of fools he had yet to see. Still, he thought it wise not to waste any more time. He had already searched the earl's study to no avail, which meant he would now start on the library. With any luck, he would find the evidence he needed to wrap the earl up in a tidy package.

He was enjoying his cigar when he sensed movement behind him. Whirling around, his knife already at the ready, he found himself staring into Lord Jonathan's dark eyes.

"Peace, Your Grace," Lord Jonathan responded with a light laugh, raising his hands above his head. "I hadn't meant to startle you. I saw you slip away from the company, and thought to join you for a smoke."

"You should know better than to creep up on people, Jonathan." Anthony's voice was dampening as he slipped the knife back into its sheath. "I could have gutted you."

"That is so," Jonathan agreed, leaning his broad shoulders against one of the stone pillars and regarding Anthony with obvious interest. "I commend you on your restraint." When Anthony didn't respond, he gave a soft chuckle. "Still the clam mouth, aren't you? You're every bit as mysterious as our distinguished leader. I don't suppose you'd care to tell me what's *really* going on here, would you?"

Anthony stiffened at the question. "I'm not

sure I know what you mean, Lord Jonathan," he
answered warily. "Perhaps you would care to explain yourself?"

"Oh, come, Marchfield." Jonathan's boyish
smile widened. "It should be obvious why I am
here. Sir sent me."

"Did he?" Anthony asked softly. "How
strange. He never bothered informing me I
should expect reinforcements."

"It was a last-minute decision. Sir is worried
about the leak in our group, and he's decided he
doesn't want anyone working alone."

That sounded plausible enough, for Sir often
went to great lengths to safeguard his men. Still,
Anthony recalled Sir's insistence that the nature
of his mission be kept secret between the two of
them. If he had seen fit to involve another agent
he would have sent word. Anthony studied Jonathan's handsome face, his eyes narrowing as he
noted the other man's coloring.

"I fail to see why a simple surveillance should
require two agents," he said, folding his arms
across his chest. "Aimsford isn't that dangerous."

"Aimsford?" Jonathan's brown eyes gleamed
speculatively. "He's the reason you're here?"

"You mean you didn't know?" Anthony raised
a dark eyebrow in surprise. "What did Sir tell
you?"

"The usual." Jonathan shrugged his shoulders,
pulling a cheroot from his pocket and lighting it
with a flint. "Nothing. I assumed you would fill
me in when I got here."

Some of the tenseness left Anthony at Jonathan's words. Sir's mania for secrecy was abso-

lute, and he never revealed one agent's assignment to another. Even if a man was captured and forced to tell all he knew, he could only betray his own mission and the few agents known to him. It had kept them alive until one agent had turned traitor. A traitor with brown eyes . . .

"How is Sir?" Anthony asked, propping his foot on a stone bench and regarding Jonathan with studied nonchalance. "He is well, I trust?"

"That's hard to say, as I haven't seen him. I received word through one of those guttersnipes he employs as couriers that I was to join you here, but that is all I do know." Jonathan stared at him pointedly.

Anthony hesitated, then launched into a false explanation for his presence at Shipton Hall. He was deliberately vague, knowing Jonathan's suspicions would be aroused if he was too forthcoming.

"That sounds like Sir," Jonathan said after Anthony had finished his story. "Only he would take such a circuitous route to achieve his objective. If that snake Aimsford is using the local gentlemen to smuggle arms to France, then he'd never suspect you of spying on him. Posing as Lady Cassandra's suitor is a brilliant disguise, Marchfield; my congratulations."

"It was Sir's idea," Anthony said, relieved Jonathan had been so quick to accept his story. "I only wish it was he who had to act out the role; it's grown damned uncomfortable. Each time the countess and her beauteous daughter look at me I feel as if I am being measured for my burial shroud!"

"Ah, yes, the threat of matrimony is an unexpected danger, is it not?" Jonathan laughed appreciatively. "You have my condolences, sir. But in the meanwhile, what can I do to be of service to you? Two pairs of eyes are much more effective than one, don't you agree?"

They spent the next half hour discussing strategy, and then Anthony took his leave. Slipping away from the garden, he made his way to the west wing of the house where the library was located. He closed the door behind him and, lighting a candle, began a methodical search. As Sir had predicted, he found the *Journals* hidden on the shelves.

Excitement flared through him as he opened the book, reading the meticulously penned lines with satisfaction. That feeling quickly turned to rage as he recognized aspects of himself in the character Lady X had dubbed "Lord Stiffback." He was so engrossed in his reading that he wasn't aware of another's presence until he heard a startled gasp.

"What are you doing with my notebook?"

He dropped the book to the floor and turned to confront the intruder. In a flash he drew the pistol from its hiding place, training it on the figure who stood in the door, regarding him with wide-eyed horror.

"Miss Malvern." He lowered the gun slowly, his eyes taking note of her white face and terrified expression. "Please don't be alarmed; it's not what you think, I promise. Come in and close the door behind you."

She stared at him in disbelief. "First I find you

snooping in my uncle's study, and now you point
a gun at me and you ask that I shut myself in
here with you?" She shook her head slowly.
"You're mad, sir, if you think I'll do as you bid!
This time, I'm telling my uncle!" She began back-
ing out the door.

He reached her in a few steps, clamping one
hand roughly over her mouth, and pulling the
door closed with the other. He dragged her into
the center of the room, his arms slipping around
her waist as he fought to control her furious attempts to free herself.

"Blast it, Jacinda, will you stop it?" he cursed,
wincing as her sharp teeth sank into the flesh of
his thumb. "I told you, it's not what you think!"

Jacinda glared at him over his hand. It was bad
enough to be caught, she fumed silently, but to
be caught by the Duke of Marchfield seemed the
ultimate insult. Then she remembered he had
been reading the *Journals* when she blundered
upon him. He had looked furious, his sensual
mouth tight with displeasure and his eyes silver
with rage. What if he had recognized himself as
Lord Stiffback? The thought was enough to make
her go still at once, humiliation and terror washing through her.

Anthony felt her relax and warily lifted his
hand, holding it poised over her lips in case she
attempted to scream a warning. When it became
evident she had no such intentions, he guided her
to a nearby chair and gently pushed her down.
"There's no need to be afraid," he said, taking her
chilled hand between his and chafing it gently. "I

mean you no harm, I promise you. But I was looking for the *Journals* and—"

"I . . . you . . . you know who Lady X is, don't you?" she demanded in a voice devoid of all hope. "You won the bet."

"You know about the bet?" He was vaguely surprised.

She nodded miserably, wondering if she should humiliate herself by throwing herself on his mercy. Perhaps if she explained that her life would be ruined if he tattled, and offered him money to replace the money he would lose in the bet, she could convince him to keep his peace. She glanced up at him through her lashes, her heart pounding with fear. "There's . . . there's no reason for you to tell, is there?" she asked, licking her lips nervously. "It seems so cruel and meaningless to destroy someone's life merely to win a bet."

"I'm not doing this because of that ridiculous bet," he said, frowning at her in confusion. "Do you mean you *know* your uncle is Lady X?" he demanded incredulously.

Now it was her turn to be confused. "My uncle?"

"I can understand your wanting to protect him," he continued, working out matters in his mind even as he spoke. Given Jacinda's quick mind it was only natural she should have tumbled to the truth, and it was equally natural that as a dutiful niece she would want to keep that knowledge to herself. He dreaded being the one to tell her that her beloved uncle was a traitor, but he had no choice.

"Yes, I've been aware for some time that your uncle is Lady X," he said, kneeling before her, clasping her hands firmly in his. "All I lacked for the final proof was a copy of the *Journals* written in his own hand. Now I have it." He nodded to the notebook lying facedown on the floral carpet.

"The final proof?" she asked, thinking that was rather an ominous way of phrasing things. "What do you mean?"

"I know this will be hard for you, Jacinda, and I truly wish I didn't have to tell you, but the simple truth is your uncle is a traitor. He's been passing secret information to the French using the *Journals*."

Jacinda could only gaze at him through dilated eyes, her mouth opening and closing several times before she managed to gasp, "You're insane! My uncle would never betray his country! He would sooner die!"

"I only wish that was so," he said in a voice made soft with pity, "but the proof is irrefutable. Were it not for the adverse publicity a trial would have upon public morale, he would be brought to trial and publicly executed. He'll be given the chance to take the honorable way out in order to spare his family further shame, but that is all I can grant him, Jacinda. I'm sorry."

She shook her head slowly, praying she had gone mad. This couldn't be happening. She looked at Marchfield's face, so grim and yet so oddly tender, and knew the moment she had been dreading for the past three years was finally upon her. She had no choice other than to tell the truth. Fighting down the fear that threatened to overcome her, she said, "My uncle is not Lady X."

"I know that is what you want to think," Anthony said, touched by her obstinate faith in her uncle. "But I told you, we have all the proof we need for a conviction. Should this go before a jury I can assure you he would be found guilty, and your entire family would be ruined."

"But he's not Lady X!" she cried, determined to be brave. "I told you, I—"

"Jacinda, I tell you that he is!" Anthony leapt to his feet, glaring down at her in exasperation. "Why won't you believe me?"

"Because, you idiot," she stormed, also leaping to her feet and meeting him glare for glare, "*I* am Lady X!"

Chapter Eight

"You're *what?*"

"I'm Lady X," Jacinda affirmed, her voice quavering as she met the duke's incredulous gaze.

Anthony shook his head, disbelieving the evidence of his own ears. "You can't be," he said slowly, struggling to make sense of what he had heard. "I know you love your uncle, Jacinda, but you can't possibly hope to protect him with this ridiculous story."

"It's not ridiculous!" she exclaimed, incipient

pique diluting the fear that was coursing through her veins.

"It is indeed," he retorted, running a hand through his thick hair. "You couldn't be responsible for this treasonous bit of trash!" He gave the offending notebook a swift kick, sending it sailing across the room to land in front of the door.

Jacinda chased after it, picking it up and clasping it protectively to her bosom. "How dare you criticize my work!" she cried as she rose to her feet. "It's not trash, and it most certainly is not treasonous! Why do you keep saying that?"

Anthony gaped at her, skepticism slowly giving way to shocked acceptance. Oddly enough it was her fierce defense of the book that convinced him. Only the real author would have defended a charge of poor writing over a charge of treason, he decided in stunned dismay.

"You're Lady X," he stated in a low voice, still struggling to come to terms with her confession.

"That's what I've been trying to tell you!" Jacinda grumbled, warily keeping her distance from him. "And I can prove it, too."

"How?"

She held up the notebook. "This is my handwriting, not my uncle's. And if you insist, I suppose I could arrange to have my publisher confirm my identity, although I should prefer that you not contact him. I have my reputation to think of, you know."

"Your reputation?" he echoed, staring at her in outrage. Had she not been listening to a single word he'd said? "My God, Jacinda, that is the least of your worries! Hasn't it sunk in yet? You're in serious trouble; you stand accused of treason!"

Her defiance vanished under the impact of his words. "But . . . but I haven't done anything!" she whispered, her face paling with horror. "You're wrong. I'd never, never betray my country!"

"But you've already done just that," Anthony said bluntly, believing her impassioned denial at once. Not that it changed things, of course, he realized, suddenly feeling very old and very tired. What the hell was he going to do with her now?

"How?" Tears stood in Jacinda's eyes as she studied Anthony's grim face. However ludicrous his charges might be, it was obvious to her that he believed them. "Please," she implored, moving to stand before him, "tell me what it is I'm supposed to have done. I don't understand any of this!"

"It's not that easy, Jacinda," Anthony said reluctantly. "But the charges have been made from . . . from somebody in a position of great power. That is why I am here. I've been assigned to find Lady X and to silence her."

If anything, Jacinda grew paler. "Are you a Bow Street Runner?"

"Not precisely. But I do act with full authority for the crown, I assure you."

She swallowed uncomfortably. He looked so rigid, she thought with growing fear, so unyielding, rather like an avenging angel. His gray eyes surveyed her with unwavering regard, and his

lean jaw was set at a determined angle. If she
thought him pompous and arrogant before this,
then that impression paled in comparison. He
looked . . . Her mind scrambled to find the correct word . . . He looked deadly.

"But what did I do?" she asked, a single tear
escaping from her eye and flowing down the
curve of her cheek.

"You really have no idea, do you?" he demanded, shaking his head in disgust. "You
blithely give away confidential information such
as troop strength and the number of men assigned to guard the king, and then have the audacity to ask what you have done? For God's
sake, Jacinda! Don't you know how dangerous
that knowledge could be in the wrong hands? In
French hands?"

"But . . . but I never knew . . . that is, I
never thought it would matter. I only put down
what I heard! How was I to know it was important?"

"You should have known it!" he snapped angrily, the ice in his eyes melting with exasperation. "You're not an idiot, Jacinda. Didn't it occur
to you that as we are at war, the last thing we
would want our enemies to know is the exact
number of men assigned to protect our cities?"

Jacinda's eyes widened in horrified comprehension. "But it was just a joke," she said weakly.
"Just a little joke. I was merely having a bit of
fun."

"Your 'bit of fun' could well have cost many
men their lives!" Anthony said harshly, enraged

that she had placed all of them in danger without even comprehending the damage she had caused. Well, by God, he would *make* her understand!

"You realize I shall have to take you into custody," he said, staring down the length of his patrician nose at her. "As an accused traitor, you can hardly be allowed to go free."

For a moment Jacinda feared she would swoon. Only her pride kept her on her feet, pride and a certain amount of outrage. She knew what she had done was wrong, very wrong indeed, but that did not give the duke the right to terrorize her. She tilted her head back, meeting his cold stare with a bravery she was far from feeling. "Do you mean to arrest me, Your Grace?" she asked with commendable control.

"Clap you in irons, do you mean?" Anthony was too angry to be impressed by her sudden show of spirit. "I should, I suppose, but I'm counting on your sense of family loyalty to keep you from bolting."

"What do you mean?"

"Merely that if you do decide to sneak off in the dead of night, you will leave me no choice but to arrest your uncle."

"But he's innocent!" Jacinda protested, furious that he should be so ruthless. "You said so yourself!"

"Not really." He was coldly pleased to see she still retained a particle of sense. "I merely agree that you are Lady X; that doesn't mean your uncle is innocent of aiding and abetting you in that treason. You had to get the information on troop strength from somewhere, and the earl is a member of the Privy Council."

"But he didn't know I was in the room! He was talking to Aunt Prudence, and I simply wrote down the figures. I mean," she added hastily, "I thought it interesting because of Lady Jersey . . . that is, because so many ladies have a fondness for men in uniform. It was an amusing trifle, nothing more."

"That has yet to be proven," he replied loftily. "In the meanwhile, I want your word that you won't disappear from the Hall until I have had the opportunity to investigate further. Do I have it?"

"Of course you have it!" she answered, fairly bristling with indignation. "I know I'm innocent, and I intend proving it to you."

"That might be somewhat difficult, considering you have already freely admitted your guilt," he said, holding his hand out commandingly. "The notebook, if you please, Miss Malvern."

That she was now Miss Malvern when only seconds earlier she had been Jacinda did not escape her notice. She clutched the journal closer. "Why?" she demanded suspiciously.

"Because it's evidence." He was unperturbed by her small act of rebellion. "It would be a pity if it was destroyed during the night . . . by accident, of course."

She thrust the notebook into his hands, glaring at him in impotent fury. "Is that all, Anthony?" she asked with false sweetness, using his Christian name in a deliberate attempt to insult him.

"Not quite. Do you have any of the other *Journals* with you? I'll need all of them."

"Of course, Anthony. If you'll wait here, I'd be happy to go and fetch them for you." She turned to leave, but he stayed her with a firm hand on her elbow.

"One moment, Miss Malvern."

"Yes?" She studied him over her shoulder.

"I'm coming with you. I'm afraid I really can't let you out of my sight until all the *Journals* have been secured."

Jacinda's jaw dropped. "I . . . but you can't come with me!" she gasped, her cheeks pinking in distress. "They're in my bedchamber!"

"So?" Anthony hid a smile at her outraged expression.

"So?" Jacinda repeated in disbelief. "So I can hardly let you in my bedchamber! It wouldn't be proper."

"It seems rather strange to me that a woman who calmly admits to committing treason should balk at the thought of entertaining a man in her private chambers," he said in a sardonic voice. "But in any case, I'm afraid I must insist. Until all the papers are safely in my hands, you aren't going anywhere. Do you understand me?"

Her eloquent glare was reply enough, and Anthony stepped aside. "After you, Jacinda, my love," he murmured, executing a mocking bow.

Much to Jacinda's relief, Anthony agreed to stay in her sitting room while she dragged her books out from their hiding place beneath her bed. In addition to the originals of the other three

Journals, she also had the rough drafts of the gothic she had been penning, and several copies of some articles she hoped to publish. She grabbed these as well, then struggled to her feet, her arms loaded down with a mountain of paper.

"Here you are, sir," she said, staggering slightly as she rejoined him in the outer room. "I hope you find everything in order." She dumped the papers into his arms.

"All of this is related to the *Journals*?" he protested, struggling to hang on to the myriad slips of papers and notebooks in his hands.

"No." She smiled at him serenely. "But I thought you would want to see everything. After all, if I betrayed England in my *Journals,* heaven only knows what I might have let slip in my gothic and my articles! Who knows what you will find once you have had the chance to go over them . . . thoroughly, and at great length." She opened the door for him. "Good night, Anthony. Happy reading."

"Curse you, Jacinda!" he hissed, his brows lowering in a threatening scowl. "You know I don't want this . . . this pile of foolscap!" He jiggled the papers in his arms, causing a few of them to flutter to the floor like snowflakes. "The only thing I'm interested in is the *Journals.*"

"Oh, they're in there . . . somewhere," she assured him with another smile. "I'm sure you'll find them eventually." And she swung the door closed in his face.

He stood staring at the sturdy-looking wood in speechless fury. Muttering an angry oath beneath his breath, he turned and stalked down the hall, leaving a trail of paper in his wake. He was so absorbed with thoughts of how he would take his revenge that he never heard the sound of another door, farther down the hall, closing quietly.

Jacinda spent a restless night alternately pacing the floor and tossing and turning in her bed. When she did manage to fall asleep, she dreamed of towering scaffolds and dark cells tucked away in crumbling castles. She rose shortly after dawn, and after washing her face in the tepid water left over from the night before, she donned her riding habit and went out to the stables.

"Good day to ye, Miss Jacinda." Chelms, the elderly groom who had been with the earl since he was a lad, greeted her with a startled look. "Ye be up with the birds this morning."

"Hello, Chelms." She gave him a tired smile. "Would you please saddle Lady Jane for me? I feel like a ride."

"Lady Jane's right foreleg be giving her fits, miss," Chelms apologized, pulling his torn cap from his head. "And none of the other horses be suitable for a lady."

Jacinda rubbed a weary hand over her burning eyes, fighting off the sudden impulse to cry. She was usually not given to such displays of feminine histrionics, but she had just passed through the worst night of her life. She had been threatened, terrorized, and humiliated, and she was all but at the end of her endurance. She wanted to ride, and by heaven, she would ride.

"Saddle up Nightwind, Chelms," she ordered, pulling her beaver hat over her forehead. "I shall take him."

"Nightwind, miss?" Chelm's pale blue eyes stared from his lined face. "Are you sure? He be a right handful."

"I'm sure." Her chin came up in determination. She was in the mood for a good fight, and if Nightwind proved to be recalcitrant, she was more than ready for him. "Please get him ready."

Chelms disappeared into the stable, scratching his head and muttering about the queer notions of the gentry folk. He returned a short time later, leading a very disgruntled Nightwind. The black horse's ears were laid back in a show of displeasure, and Jacinda could swear there was a pout on his equine face.

"I don't rightly know about this, Miss Jacinda," Chelms said as he helped her mount. "Nightwind's not used to a sidesaddle, and he's in a temper this morning from the looks of him. Mayhap I should fetch you a different horse, eh? How about Dandy Fellow?"

"No, Nightwind and I will suit each other quite well, Chelms, thank you," Jacinda said, wrapping the reins around her wrist, and pulling back on the bridle. "He might be in a temper, but so am I." She touched her tiny spurs to the horse's muscular flanks, and they took off across the pasture toward the cliffs.

At first, Jacinda feared she wouldn't be able to keep her seat. Nightwind was full of the devil, and he tried every trick known to horse and man to toss her from his back. But when it became evident that his rider's determination matched his own, he gave up the struggle and poured his champion's heart into running as fast as he could. They reached the cliff in half the usual time, and Jacinda's heart was pounding with fear and exhilaration as she reined him in.

"Well done, Nightwind!" she gasped, leaning over to give his neck an affectionate pat. "I think we understand each other now, don't we?"

Nightwind blew noisily, jangling the bridle as he shook his head. Jacinda nudged him toward one of the large rocks that had been placed there centuries before by a provident act of nature and carefully dismounted. Tying the reins to the branches of a nearby tree, she turned and gazed at the sea that stretched out before her.

The ride had chased away the last vestige of weariness from her brain, and as she took a deep, cleansing breath of salt air, Jacinda reached the decision that had been plaguing her all night. Upon her return, she would go to her uncle and confess all.

It was the only way, she decided, settling the green skirts of her habit about her as she knelt on the dew-damp grass. He would be furious, of course, and in all likelihood he would show her the door. But in the end, it would all be for the best. In the event the duke went through with his bullying threats and had her arrested, then at the very least she could spare the family the humiliation of a trial.

She crossed her arms over her folded knees, resting her chin against the soft tarlatan as she contemplated her bleak future. She would have to migrate, of course, provided that she wasn't transported. Or worse. Her brow puckered in thought. What was the penalty for accidental treason?

"What the devil do you mean you let her take Nightwind?" Anthony demanded, glowering at the nervous groom through narrowed gray eyes. "That beast is no fit mount for a lady!"

"I know that, Your Grace." Chelms twisted his hat in gnarled hands as he faced the duke. "I tried telling Miss Jacinda as much, but she wouldn't listen! " 'Saddle up Nightwind, Chelms,' she said, and there weren't a blamed thing I could do."

"Which direction did they take?" Anthony asked, anxiously scanning the horizon for any sign of a horse and rider. According to the stable hand, Jacinda had left less than five minutes ago. They should still be somewhere in sight.

"That way, Your Grace." Chelms jerked a grubby thumb toward the cliffs. "She took off on that black devil like she was a part of him, and him doing everything he could to throw her."

Anthony's mouth hardened at this bit of news. "Did it look as if she had him in control?" he asked, tugging on his leather gloves.

"Well, she was still a'top of him last I seen of 'em," Chelms volunteered with a shrug. "If you means to catch up with 'em I'd best fetch the Sheik for you. He be the only stallion we got that can keep up with Nightwind."

"Then fetch him, blast it!" Anthony ordered between clenched teeth, fighting off the nameless terror that had assailed him the moment he learned what Jacinda had done.

Curse the obstreperous female, anyway, he thought, pacing up and down the stable yard as he awaited the groom's return. Could she never once do the proper thing? He had spent the greater part of last evening poring over the pile of paper she had fobbed off on him, and he'd reached the conclusion that she was indeed innocent of any wrongdoing. Now all that remained was convincing Sir of the fact.

"Here you go, Your Grace." Chelms shuffled forward with a dun-colored Arabian. "If you're in a hurry you might cut through the east pasture. That'll take you right to the cliffs without going through the forest."

"She rode Nightwind through the forest?" Anthony gasped, paling at the mental image of Jacinda being brushed from the charging stallion's back by a low-hanging branch.

"Last I saw they was. But that ain't to say they didn't double back through the meadow. Takes a bit more time, but it's a world safer. If Miss Jacinda had anything to say 'bout it, that's the way she'd have gone."

"Then that's the way I'll go," Anthony decided, springing into the saddle and taking the reins in his capable hands. "If I'm not back with Miss Jacinda within the hour I want you to get the other hands and begin a thorough search. And Chelms?" The silky note in his cold voice made the groom shift warily.

"Yes, Your Grace?"

"God help you if she's been hurt."

Anthony followed Jacinda's trail through the meadow. As it was still early in the morning the hoofprints left by Nightwind were clearly visible in the soft grass, and the pile of manure he found was fresh enough to reassure him that he couldn't be very far behind the horse and his rider.

He burst over the crest of the hill, drawing Sheik to a plunging halt and glancing wildly around him. He spied Nightwind almost at once, contentedly munching the leaves of the tree to which he had been tied. But of Jacinda, there was no sign. Then a movement on the very edge of the cliff caught his eye.

"My God!" he whispered hoarsely, fear and horror constricting his heart. "No!" And he laid his whip across the stallion's back. "Jacinda!" he shouted, guiding his mount toward the slender figure standing poised at the very edge of the cliff. "Stop!"

The sound of her name being shouted penetrated Jacinda's thoughts, and she glanced up in surprise to see Anthony racing toward her at breakneck speed. She barely had time to note he was riding Sheik when he stopped scarcely three feet from where she was standing.

"Jacinda, come away from there!" Anthony called out, leaping from the horse and coming toward her, his hands outstretched in supplication. "This is not the answer. Come away from there, and we'll talk, I promise you."

Jacinda frowned at him in confusion. Really, he was the strangest man. What on earth could he be thinking of to ride a horse so close to the edge of the cliff? He might have been killed.

"Anthony?" His name sprang unbidden to Jacinda's lips as she stared at him. "What are you doing here?"

"I decided to take a morning ride," Anthony replied, inching closer. Keep her talking, he thought desperately, keep her talking. "If I'd known you were going out as well, I'd have risen earlier. You should have waited."

"I wanted to be alone." Jacinda turned away from him, gazing down at the waves slapping against the shore. It was low tide, and the large rocks jutted high above the wet, hard-packed sand. "I needed to decide what I should do about the *Journals*," she continued in a pensive voice, folding her arms across her chest. "But there's really only one thing I can do . . . isn't there?"

"No, there are always other options." Anthony stopped less than an arm's length from her, afraid that if he came any closer he would drive her over the edge. He wet his lips nervously. "Jacinda, I know that right now this must look like the only solution, but it's not. Come away from there, and we'll find some other way out of this."

"But I thought you would be pleased," she said, more baffled than ever by his odd behavior. "It's the best for all concerned and—"

He leapt forward without warning, grabbing her by the waist and flinging her bodily away from the cliff's edge. His unexpected movement startled her, and her hands clutched instinctively at the front of his jacket. Their combined momentum was enough to overset Anthony, and they went tumbling to the ground in a tangle of arms and legs. Anthony expertly rolled to one side, taking the brunt of the fall, and they came to rest with Jacinda pinned beneath him.

"Have you gone mad?" she gasped once she'd regained the breath that had been knocked from her. "Let me up at once!" She swung her fist at his jaw.

He easily avoided the blow, capturing both of her small hands in his and pinning them above her head. "I'm trying to save your life!" he rasped, glaring down at her through narrowed silver eyes.

"You *are* mad," she announced with conviction, fighting to dislodge him. "For the last time, will you let me up!"

"Why?" Anthony demanded arrogantly, ignoring her futile struggles. "So you can leap from the cliff like some heroine out of one of your silly gothics? Oh, no, Miss Malvern, if you think I'll let you take the coward's way out, then you are much mistaken!"

Jacinda went still at his words. "You thought . . . you thought I meant to *kill* myself?" she squeaked in disbelief.

He nodded his head in agreement, a lock of dark hair falling across his tanned forehead. "It's rather obvious, isn't it? First you go haring off on a horse you had no hopes of controlling, and when I finally find you you're standing on the edge of a cliff. What else was I to think?"

"Sometimes, Your Grace, I wonder if you ever do think!" she shot back, scowling up at him. "First you claim my dull-witted uncle is Lady X, and in the next breath you accuse me of being a

French spy. Now you say that I am so foolish as to want to kill myself!" Her hazel eyes raked over him with obvious derision. "And they say women have overly fanciful imaginations!"

Anthony's lips thinned at her sneering words. "Then you weren't going to jump?" he asked suspiciously.

"Of course I wasn't!" Her hat had been knocked askew in the fall, and the once-jaunty feather dangled in front of one eye. She blew it away, her eyes taking on a militant gleam as they met Anthony's. "I can assure you, Your Grace, that had I intended for one of us to go sailing off that cliff it most assuredly would *not* have been me!"

"You wouldn't be the first to prefer suicide to disgrace," he said, helping her to her feet. "In fact, that's the way we prefer to settle things."

She slapped his hands away. "What do you mean?"

"Merely that in such cases as yours, the traitor is offered one of two choices." Anthony spoke without thinking. "Either he faces a public trial and the ruination of his family and his good name or . . ."

"Or what?"

Anthony rolled his eyes heavenward as if seeking divine guidance. Jacinda was without doubt the most difficult, most obstinate female it had ever been his misfortune to encounter. He placed his hands on his hips, his gaze holding hers as he answered bluntly, "Or a loaded pistol and a locked room. Need I elaborate further?"

Jacinda's eyes widened in comprehension, her

writer's mind painting an all too graphic picture. "Do you . . . . do you mean I will have to shoot myself?" she gasped in disbelief, her eyes filling with tears. *Good Lord,* she thought with mounting horror, even leaping from the cliff would be preferable to that!

"Of course not!" He seemed as appalled as she by the notion.

"But you just said—"

"I didn't mean you!" Anthony exclaimed in exasperation, his hands descending on her shoulders and administering a none too gentle shake. "I was talking about *real* traitors, men who sell their country for personal profit!"

"But that's what you think I did." She blinked back tears of fright. "You said someone . . . someone of great importance told you to find and . . . and silence me."

Anthony's expression grew grim as he thought of Sir. He'd lain awake wondering what his superior would do in his place. Jacinda was Lady X, that was true, but she was hardly the cold-blooded traitor he had been expecting. Her crime was one of ignorance, but it was still a crime, and it carried the heaviest penalty of the law. Legally, Jacinda was guilty of treason against the crown. Morally . . .

"I could speak to him," he said slowly, meeting Jacinda's wide hazel eyes. "Perhaps if I explain that you meant no harm, that you didn't realize what you were doing, he would be willing to forget the matter."

"Do you really think he would do that?"

Jacinda asked, a faint flame of hope beginning to flicker inside her.

"He might." Anthony wished he could be more positive, but Sir was a law unto himself, with a rigid code of honor. If Jacinda's innocent tattling had cost even one English life, he might be merciless. "But I'll try, Jacinda. I swear to heaven, I will try."

Her head dropped to his shoulder, and her eyes closed wearily. "I'm sorry, Anthony," she whispered softly. "I'm so very sorry."

"I know." He slipped his arms about her, holding her in a tender embrace. "You're a hellcat and a termagant, but I know you would never willingly betray anyone."

She smiled at the teasing words as if they were the sweetest of accolades. Held close to him like this she could feel the warmth of his flesh through his jacket, and catch the faintest scent of his spicy cologne. Part of her was shocked that she would notice such things, but the secret, most feminine part was delighted, and urged her on to further indiscretions. She tipped her head back, her light brown hair tumbling free from its bun and streaming over his arm as she smiled up at him.

"You're being most generous, Your Grace," she told him in an unconsciously seductive voice. "Considering the trick I played on you."

Anthony's eyes moved over her upturned face, coming to rest on the moist provocation of her gently parted lips. "Ah, but you have played so many tricks on me these past few weeks, my dear Miss Malvern, that I'm not certain what you mean. Are you referring, perhaps, to the time you threw the sherry in my face? Or last night when you loaded me down with enough paper to sink a frigate? Or . . ." He paused, his silver eyes taking on a knowing gleam. "Or using me as the pattern card for your newest hero, Lord Stiffback?"

Jacinda pulled back, a delicate blush stealing over her cheeks as she gazed up at him. "You mean you know?" she gasped in mortification.

"Mmm." He smiled down at her. "And might I say that my voice is most assuredly not nasal. Nor do I stutter."

"Oh, those were simply characteristics I threw in to be amusing," she assured him hastily. "But the rest—"

"The rest is a wicked, and I fear, rather accurate depiction of the face I choose to show society. My congratulations, Lady X, your pen is as unerringly accurate as ever."

"Please don't call me that," she implored, shuddering with distaste. "When I think of the mischief I have caused with those wretched *Journals,* I vow I feel quite ill."

"Actually, I rather enjoyed them," he said, guiding her toward the horses. "Especially your latest work. It should make quite a stir when it's published."

"But I'm not going to publish it," she protested, turning around to face him. "I can't . . . can I?"

"Perhaps, once it has been cleansed of all sensitive information," he replied, considering the matter carefully. "You really have a very sharp

ear, Jacinda. It appalls me when I realize how loose-tongued people have been with our country's most sensitive secrets. It's a wonder Boney hasn't defeated us long before now." He gave her a thoughtful look. "Which reminds me, how the devil did you learn of Sir? I would have sworn he was the best-kept secret in the country."

"Who is Sir?" She accepted his help mounting Nightwind. "I'm afraid I don't know who you're talking about."

"The group of spies surrounding the Prince Regent. You mentioned them in your last book." Anthony thrust his foot in the stirrup, swinging his leg over Sheik's back.

"I was talking about Lady Jersey and Lady Hertford." Jacinda cast him a puzzled glance. "Everyone knows they are the worst gossips in the country, and that the prince uses them so he might be kept au courant of the latest scandals. Who did you think I meant?"

"No one." He gave her an angelic smile, although privately he felt like laughing. To think both he and Sir had been thrown into a panic at the thought of their organization being uncovered, and the whole time she was talking about two aging, overpainted gossips!

They rode back toward Shipton Hall in silence, both lost in their private musings. They were cutting through the meadow when Jacinda finally spoke. "Well, I suppose I should go and find my uncle. The sooner I tell him that I am Lady X, the sooner I can be on my way."

"What on earth are you talking about?"

"Well," she said, determined to be practical despite her trepidation, "you really don't think he'll let me stay once the truth is out, do you? I shall be fortunate if he doesn't set the dogs on me as well."

"Why the devil should you tell him you're Lady X?" Anthony demanded, his brows meeting in a frown.

"It's bound to come out," she replied stoically, her hands clenching on the reins and causing Nightwind to dance in annoyance. "You might be willing to hold your tongue for the moment, but what about the others? There's the bet, remember, and once they learn that I'm Lady X, my reputation will be in tatters! The very least I can do is spare my aunt and uncle the humiliation."

"By confessing to something they may never even know?" he argued, his jaw coming forward pugnaciously. "What makes you think that pack of dandies will learn the truth? *I'm* a trained spy, and I never once suspected you! If you managed to cozen me, then you may rest assured they'll never even guess."

"Perhaps not, but—"

"But nothing, Jacinda. You're not telling your uncle you're Lady X, and that's final."

Chapter Nine

Anthony left Jacinda in the stables and hurried up to his rooms to change for breakfast. He glanced at the papers on his dressing table as he walked past it, thinking he'd need to go through them again before contacting Sir. Perhaps if he sent portions of her new book he could prove Jacinda innocent of any malevolence. He turned toward his wardrobe, his hands tugging his stock, when he stopped abruptly.

He swung back, his eyes going over the pile of papers with professional scrutiny. When he'd left, one of the notebooks, bound neatly in blue leather, had been lying on top of the papers. Now it was gone. He began searching through the papers, tossing them to the ground in his haste, but in the end his suspicions were confirmed. The *Journals* and every scrap of paper pertaining to them were missing.

For a moment he simply stood there, stunned and sickened by his discovery. The *Journals* had been there when he'd left for his ride, meaning the theft had occurred some time within the last hour. He wasn't usually so careless with valuable evidence, but as no one knew he had the *Journals,* he'd felt no need to secure them.

He didn't waste any time speculating as to whether or not one of the servants might have taken them while cleaning the room. For security reasons, his valet kept his rooms for him, and John was too well trained to disturb his personal effects. That left only one person who had both a strong motive and a houseful of accomplices eager to help her. Without giving the matter any further thought, he stormed out of his room.

He had spent his first week at Shipton Hall learning the lay of the house, and he knew where every member of the household slept. Avoiding the rooms where the guests were staying, he went directly to Jacinda's rooms, throwing the door open with such force that it bounced off the wall.

"Where the devil are my *Journals*?"

The plump maid assisting Jacinda clapped her hands over her mouth, her dark eyes wide with shock. Jacinda whirled around at his entrance, still wearing her riding habit, although she had removed the jacket. "What on earth are you bellowing about now?" she demanded indignantly. "And what do you mean by barging into my room like—"

"The *Journals,* Jacinda," he said, advancing on her in a menacing fashion. "Where are they?"

"How should I know?" she exclaimed, refusing to be cowed by his fury. "I gave them to you last night, if you'll recall and . . ." Her hazel eyes grew round at the obvious conclusion to his accusations. "Oh, my heavens, do you mean to say that *you* don't have them?"

Her expression of utter dismay convinced him of her innocence as nothing else could have. His anger cooled as quickly as it had flared as he realized she hadn't betrayed him. He flicked a glance at the hovering maid, who was listening to the exchange with avid interest. "You may go," he ordered tersely.

"Oh, but, Your Grace, that ain't proper!" she

protested in shocked tones. "I can't leave Miss Jacinda alone in her room with a man! It—"

"I said, you may go."

The maid heard the quiet command in his voice and scurried past him, her outrage evident in the stiff set of her round shoulders.

"You really don't have the *Journals*?" Jacinda asked once they were alone.

Anthony shook his head. "They were gone when I returned from our ride," he said, walking over to the french doors that led from her blue and rose sitting room to a small balcony. He pulled aside the sheer pink drapes, noting absently that although his rooms overlooked the broad meadows, hers had a view of the garden.

"And naturally you came storming in here to demand their immediate return." She laughed with wry amusement. "Tell me, sir, are all spies as volatile as you? I vow, you leap to conclusions sooner than any man I have ever met."

"It's the effect you have upon me," he replied, his lips twisting in a rueful smile. "I'm usually a model of cool restraint and propriety. And I'll thank you, ma'am, not to mention my profession again. It's supposed to be a secret."

"As you say, Your Grace. I'll try not to notice the next time I catch you ferreting through my uncle's desk." The light faded from her hazel eyes as the seriousness of the situation hit her. "Oh, Anthony, what are we going to do? Whoever has the *Journals* knows I'm Lady X. I'll be ruined."

"No you won't," he said, crossing the room and taking her hands in his. "I won't let that happen, Jacinda, I promise you. Besides, the *Journals* were found in my room, and if need be, I'll simply claim that I am Lady X. And if anyone should dispute the matter, I'll call him out."

"But you can't shoot someone for telling the truth!" she gasped, horrified at such ruthlessness.

"I won't kill him," he promised, tucking a curl behind her ear. The white ruffled blouse she was wearing clung to her gentle curves, making him burningly aware of her soft femininity. The light lilac fragrance she wore teased his nostrils, and he became acutely aware that her nearness was beginning to have an unmistakable effect upon him.

"Leave it to me, Jacinda," he said somewhat gruffly, his hands dropping to his sides as he turned away from her. "I'll think of something."

Jacinda watched him through her lowered lashes, aware of a new and exciting tension that permeated the room. She knew that the longer he remained in the room, the greater the risk of scandal should he be discovered. She opened her mouth to tell him to leave when a sudden thought occurred to her.

"Anthony," she began tentatively, "does anyone here know about you? About what you are?"

He thought immediately of Jonathan and the marquess. He couldn't identify Jonathan as a fellow agent, and he was reluctant to tell her what he knew of Aimsford. "Not to the best of my knowledge," he said evasively. "Why?"

"Well." She nibbled on her lip thoughtfully. "What if someone *does* know? Isn't it possible he might have taken the *Journals* without really knowing what they were?"

"Perhaps," he conceded with a heavy frown. "It wouldn't be the first time my rooms have been searched, although"—he rolled his shoulders in chagrin—"it is the first time anything of value has been taken. But at the moment there's really no definite way we can be certain."

"Yes, but if the person who took the *Journals* took them to prove Lady X's identity, then won't he produce them at the earliest possible opportunity?" she pressed, warming to her theme. "And if he doesn't . . ."

"If he doesn't," Anthony concluded with a slow smile, "then we have to wonder why he took them in the first place. Congratulations, Jacinda, your logic is impeccable!"

"Thank you, Your Grace," she said, pleased with his praise. "I do try."

"I'm beginning to think you may have missed your calling," he said, giving her a teasing wink. "With your devious frame of mind and unquestioned talent for eavesdropping, you would make a perfect spy! What a pity Sir refuses to recruit women as agents; you would be a valuable asset."

"A great pity, indeed," she agreed with a laugh. "You know, Anthony, I should like to meet this Sir of yours. He sounds quite fascinating."

"He is," Anthony assured her. "And speaking of Sir, something has just occurred to me. Since I can't in all good conscience hand you over to him, then it might be provident to have someone to offer in your stead."

"What do you mean?" she asked in a puzzled voice.

"Merely that Sir will be far more inclined to

overlook your little . . . shall we say indiscretion, if I complete at least part of my mission. I was sent to Shipton Hall to uncover a spy operating at the highest level of society, and so I shall. If we're right, and whoever took those *Journals* is aware of my true identity, then we can only conclude that he is also a spy . . . an enemy spy. And I'll catch him, Jacinda."

Breakfast was without doubt the longest meal Jacinda had ever endured in her two and twenty years of life. She sat at her usual place at the table waiting tensely for someone to leap to his feet, announcing he had discovered Lady X's identity. Her nerves were so strained that eating was impossible, and she spent the meal moving her serving of kippers from one side of the plate to the other. She hoped she had succeeded in hiding her agitation from the other guests, when she noted Lord Jonathan studying her.

"Do try the kidneys, Miss Malvern," he offered in a kindly tone. "They're really quite good."

"Thank you, my lord," she replied. "I'll be sure to pass your comments on to our cook. But I'm afraid I'm really not very hungry this morning."

Anthony, who had been sitting at the far end of the table politely flirting with Cassandra, glanced up at hearing Jonathan's words. His eyes flickered to Jacinda's plate and his brows lowered in a disapproving frown.

"You must eat something, Miss Malvern," he reproved her in a stern voice. "You hardly touched your food last night, and after our ride this morning, I'm certain you must be famished. If you don't want the kidneys, try the beefsteak."

Aware that she was now the center of attention, Jacinda bared her teeth in a determined smile. "Your Grace is very kind, but as I told Lord Jonathan, I'm not hun—"

Anthony turned to the footman standing behind his chair. "Bring Miss Malvern a beefsteak," he ordered crisply. "And while you're about it, fetch her some fresh tea as well. Hers is probably tepid by now."

While the footman rushed to do the duke's bidding, Jacinda contemplated dumping that tepid tea all over Anthony's head. But a strong sense of self-preservation kept her in her chair. She turned her attention back to her plate, but if she thought she would be left in peace, she was sorely disappointed.

"Personally, I find much to recommend in Miss Jacinda's regimen," Peter announced in his languid fashion. "A mouthful of food here, a sip of tepid tea there, that's all anybody really needs. Look at Byron. All he ever drinks is vinegar and water, or so he would have us believe."

"Surely you're not implying that *you* follow Miss Malvern's example?" Mr. Kirkbridge, one of the gentlemen invited down from London, hooted at Peter in good-natured derision. "I've seen you eat, Blakely, and you can tuck into your victuals the same as any man. It's a wonder you ain't burst your stays!" And he gave a loud crack of laughter.

."No true gentleman of fashion would ever resort to stays, Kirkbridge," Peter sniffed, shuddering in mock horror. "That is something which is better left to rustics and overly plump grand dames . . . or Prinny, of course, which is all very much the same thing. But for your information, I never claimed that I followed Miss Jacinda's eminently sensible advice; I merely stated that I agreed with it. 'Tis a pity others don't follow her example." His gaze rested pointedly on Kirkbridge's double chin.

This sparked a lively discussion of the latest rumors concerning the brooding poet and Brummell as well, whom, Peter claimed, bathed his face in buttermilk, which seemed to him a most ingenious use for so loathsome a commodity. When she had finished her breakfast, including the beefsteak, Jacinda rose to her feet and, after shooting Anthony one final glare, excused herself.

After leaving the morning room Jacinda went directly to the small study that had been set aside for her use at the Hall. The rosewood desk was overflowing with menus and plans for a ball that was scheduled to be held in less than a week. Cassandra was supposed to be helping her, but her petulant cousin was much more interested in gossiping with her friends and flirting with the duke to be of much assistance. Jacinda opened the doors leading to the terrace, admitting the gentle breeze blowing in from the sea. The tang of salt in the flower-scented air reminded her of those moments on the cliff when she had lain in Anthony's arms, feeling the warm strength of his body pressed to hers.

Her cheeks grew warm at the sensual memory

and the emotions she had experienced lying in Anthony's arms. Despite her anger and embarrassment she hadn't been afraid, sensing that he would never harm her. Anthony was many things, but above all else he was a gentleman. So why did she tremble now at the very memory of his touch?

It was impossible, Jacinda brooded, resting her forehead against the cool pane of glass. She was a sensible female, after all, a writer who would soon be earning her own way in the world. This was her dream, her life's ambition, and she refused to risk it all merely because of some weak, feminine notion. With that thought firmly in mind, Jacinda returned to her desk to finish the last of the invitations.

Over the next week Jacinda and Anthony saw little of each other. At first he thought it was by her design, but it soon became apparent that Lady Shipton was responsible for Jacinda's increased duties. When she wasn't busy seeing to the daily running of the household, then she was off with the steward visiting the tenants. Any hopes he might have had of visiting with her in the evenings were again thwarted by the countess, who insisted upon recruiting Jacinda to play the pianoforte for the other guests, or asking her to make up the numbers for a game of whist.

But winning time alone with Jacinda wasn't Anthony's only concern. When several days passed without anyone's stepping forward with the *Journals,* he knew he could no longer ignore the obvious. There was indeed a spy operating under his very nose, and he had a sinking suspicion who that spy might be.

Because of his doubts he decided to write to Sir, hoping the letter would somehow be delivered to him. In the terse note he detailed his suspicions, asking that Sir contact him at once with instructions. He also added the information that Jacinda was Lady X, but that she was innocent of any maleficence. Hopefully, in light of his discovery, Sir would agree to let the matter of Lady X drop. But if not, Anthony was fully prepared to fight for Jacinda's freedom.

Two days before the ball was to take place he was sitting in the library reading when Wilmount entered and paused in front of his chair. "I say, Marchfield," he began, clearing his throat nervously, "you ain't Catholic, are you?"

"I beg your pardon?" Anthony asked, glancing up with a frown. He'd already concluded that Wilmount was a dolt, an impression the viscount had done little to alter.

"Wouldn't have thought it," Wilmount continued in his ponderous way. "I mean, you are a peer, aren't you? And a member of the House of Lords. Can't sit in Parliament if—"

"Lord Shipton," Anthony interrupted in exasperation, "might I ask what the point of your ridiculous question might be? Providing, of course, that there *is* a point?"

"Well, really, Your Grace!" Wilmount drew his portly body up in indignation. "No need to take m'head off. And when you think about it, m'question makes perfect sense. It's not every day a monk comes to our door asking for a duke, and—"

"There's a monk at your door asking for me?"

"That's what I've been trying to tell you!" Wilmount's bottom lip protruded sullenly. "At least I *think* he's a monk. All dressed in brown, at any rate, and wearing one of those blasted crucifixes. Since the crown saw fit to stick those Frenchie prisoners near Dover, we've got priests and the like everywhere you look. Can't swing a cat without hitting one. They come to the back-door begging for bread sometimes, but this is the first time one of 'em has ever come into the kitchens asking to speak to one of our guests."

"I see," Anthony said, a suspicion forming slowly in his mind. "Well, in that case, perhaps I should go see what he wants." He set the book aside and rose to his feet. "He is in the kitchen, you say?"

"The footman says Cook was giving him a bit of bread and milk," Wilmount replied, trailing at Anthony's heels as he hurried toward the kitchen. "But why should a monk want to speak with you, eh? Dashed queer, if you ask me."

Anthony managed to refrain from retorting that no one had asked him, but aloud he said, "I daresay the good father wishes me to translate for him. I do speak French, you know."

"Do you?" Wilmount scratched his head. "Never could understand a word of it m'self. I always thought it a dashed waste of time learning to speak all that rot, especially as we are at war with 'em."

"A highly patriotic sentiment, sir," Anthony

replied, wondering how he could rid himself of Wilmount in the event his suspicions were confirmed. "However, in this case it might prove provident that someone here is fluent in the language."

"What do you mean?"

"Well . . . escapes aren't unheard of, you know," Anthony said, inventing his story as they hurried along the passage leading to the kitchens. "The monk might have come to warn us of such an event. Perhaps you should go and check your stables to see if all your horses are accounted for. Such a bounty would be irresistible for an escaped prisoner, don't you think?"

"M'father's Thoroughbreds?" Wilmount skittered to a halt, his plump face reddening in outrage. "Just let one of them frogs try to take one of our horses! He'll wish himself in Hades before I finish with him!" And he turned and ran back down the hall, calling out for the footman in a loud voice.

The monk sitting at the table, silently partaking of the meal served him by a giggling maid, was an older man with stooped shoulders and a full, graying beard. Anthony was beginning to doubt his instincts when the man raised his head, and his eyes were met by a familiar blue gaze.

"Good afternoon, Father," Anthony greeted the monk respectfully, allowing just the slightest note of confusion to creep into his voice. "I was told you had asked to speak with me. Might I ask what this concerns?"

"Indeed, my son," the monk replied in a heavy French accent. "I am Brother Peter, from the prison at Dover. I come on a matter of Christian charity. You speak Italian, yes? One of the guards, a Captain Weller, said that you did. He is your cousin, *non*?"

"Yes, he is," Anthony responded, wondering how Sir had learned his aunt's youngest son had been attached to the garrison at Dover. If their conversation was being overheard by someone other than the gawking servants, then this bit of information could be easily confirmed.

"Bon." The monk nodded. "Your cousin says that you speak many languages, including French and Italian, and that you are a good Christian."

"Yes?" To any unseen listeners, Anthony would appear impatient, perhaps even a little haughty with the foreign monk. If he was too friendly or overeager, suspicions were bound to be aroused.

"There is a prisoner, an Italian officer captured in Spain; he is dying, monsieur, and he wishes to write his poor wife a letter." The monk held his hands out in a pleading gesture. "Usually this is a task that I, his spiritual adviser, would be happy to undertake. But alas, his French is as poor as my Italian, and I cannot. He is too weak, and cannot write it himself. So I come to you, hoping that as a good Christian you will agree to do this small thing. Please, monsieur, in Christ's name . . . ?"

Anthony pretended to consider the request. "I'm not sure that I should," he said after a long moment. "This man is an enemy, after all, and—"

"Of course he will do it, Father." A soft voice cut into his reply, and he turned to find Jacinda standing behind him, hands on her hips as she glared at him.

"Now see here, Miss Malvern," he bristled, thanking whatever providence had brought Jacinda here. "This is none of your concern, and I'll thank you to—"

"A man is dying, Your Grace," Jacinda shot back, furious that Anthony could be so callous to the suffering of another. "I should hardly think that his nationality matters now."

"Perhaps not to you," he said in his haughtiest, most infuriating tone, "but then, you're not the one who has been asked to go into that filthy pesthole, are you? Perhaps if the situation was reversed you wouldn't be so eager to offer unsolicited advice." He deliberately turned his shoulder on her, waiting for the explosion he was sure would come.

"If I were asked, I certainly wouldn't waste precious time standing around and arguing!" Jacinda snapped, her hazel eyes narrowing on him. "I would consider it my Christian duty to help that poor man." She stalked around Anthony, her chin coming up militantly as she confronted him. "I would do as much for any man, even you, if, as you say, the situation was reversed. He's not asking you to help him escape, for pity's sake! He wants you to help him write a letter, a simple letter to his beloved wife. Is that so terrible?" Her eyes sparkled with unshed tears at the thought.

Anthony was enraptured by Jacinda's impassioned words and the emotion he saw glowing in her eyes. He knew she was probably thinking the worst of him, and there was no way he could reassure her without exposing Sir. Promising himself he would explain all to her once this was settled, he turned to Sir, who was sitting quietly at the table. "How long will this take?" he asked with obvious resignation.

"Three hours, perhaps four," the monk said, clearly relieved at the duke's words. "We must first reach the prison. I walked most of the way here, but in a carriage . . ." He shrugged his shoulders in a purely Gallic gesture.

"Miss Malvern, may I count on you to have a carriage made ready?" Anthony requested brusquely. "And also I would appreciate it if you would enclose a hamper of food. I shall undoubtedly miss my dinner."

"Yes, Your Grace," Jacinda replied, stepping around him to give the monk a warm smile. "And I'll be sure there is enough food for the father as well."

"Merci, mademoiselle." The monk crossed himself with a benign smile. "You are a credit to our Lord. God bless you."

"You're welcome, Father." Jacinda gave Anthony a smile of triumph. "At least some of us know our duty." And with that she turned and hurried from the kitchen.

"So that was Lady X," Sir remarked half an hour later as they were rolling down the road toward Dover. "She is an ape leader, isn't she?"

"A regular virago," Anthony agreed, a pleased smile touching his lips. "But you must admit her interference was fortuitous. Not even the most suspicious soul could blame me for accompanying you after that little display."

"That's true," Sir responded, scratching at his false beard. "Is she always so managing?"

"As I said, a regular virago." Anthony leaned back against the cushions, slanting a curious glance at the other man. "Am I permitted to ask why you are here? I thought you had gone into hiding?"

"I did," Sir replied calmly. "But apparently I hid too well."

"No one came looking?"

"No one even seemed to notice I was missing." His lips turned down in a mocking grimace. "It was most lowering, Marchfield, I promise you. Not even my new *petite amie* seemed to remark upon my absence."

"Madame Bouchett?" Anthony asked, raising a glass of wine to his lips. When he and Sir entered the carriage he found not one but two well-stocked hampers along with several blankets and some medical supplies. There was also a note from Jacinda to Brother Peter, asking him to put the items to their best use. Her efficiency impressed him, almost as much as the spirit of defiance with which he was sure she had placed the hampers in the coach.

"The same." Sir was also enjoying the wine, as well as some of the joint of beef and the fresh cheese. "Speaking of Daphne, I finally learned what attraction she holds for Shipton . . . above the obvious, that is. She's his financial adviser."

"His what?" Anthony almost choked on a mouthful of wine.

"His financial adviser," Sir repeated, grinning at Anthony's stunned expression. "Beneath that artfully dyed blond hair and expertly painted face, she has as sharp a financial mind it has ever been my pleasure to encounter. She's made a fortune for each of her protectors, which is rather an interesting turn, don't you think? She even made a tidy profit with the money I gave her to invest for me."

"Then she's the 'convenient relation' who keeps popping off?" Anthony was incredulous. "Why didn't he just say so?"

"What? A peer of the realm admit he keeps a French mistress who knows more about investments than he does? Use your head, Marchfield. Shipton's pride would never stand for such a thing. Besides, as a member of Parliament and the Privy Council there are some investments it's not wise for him to make. Madame Bouchett, however, suffers from no such restrictions."

"There is nothing illegal about her activities?"

"A trifle shady, perhaps," Sir allowed, shrugging philosophically. "But nothing we need concern ourselves with. And as I said, Daphne has an uncanny head for such things. If the drink or the pox doesn't kill her she'll probably become the richest woman in England, marry some destitute lord, and retire to a life of dull respectability in the country."

They drove for several more miles as Anthony digested what Sir had told him. Finally he gave a loud sigh.

"Well, I certainly made a cake of myself with this one, didn't I?" he said with a harsh laugh. "I was so sure Shipton was our man. I had all the evidence, and it fit so perfectly. Thank God we waited before taking any action." He studied Sir beneath half-lowered lashes. "I shouldn't blame you if you were to lose all faith in me, Sir."

"Why?" Sir cocked an artfully colored eyebrow at him. "I'm the one who sent you scurrying off on your fool's errand. If I hadn't leapt to the conclusion that Lady X's *Journals* were traitorous, none of this would have happened. His Highness is most amused, I assure you. I doubt he will ever let me live it down."

"You told the prince?"

"In light of what was happening I thought it best." Sir's grin was lost in the mass of his false beard. "If you hadn't flushed out the real spy, we'd all be in the soup by now."

"Is that why you're here?"

"Partially. First I want to assure you the axe man won't be polishing his blade in anticipation of whacking off Miss Malvern's lovely head. Good writers are so hard to find these days; it would be a great pity to eliminate one because of a slight case of espionage."

"And the other reason?" Anthony tensed slightly, knowing what Sir's answer would be even before he spoke.

"You're right, Anthony." Sir's blue eyes met Anthony's steady gaze. "It's Grayson."

"That bastard!" Anthony's lips twisted with hatred at the thought of the man who had betrayed his friends into the hands of the enemy. "I'll kill him!"

"Eventually," Sir agreed coolly. "But not just

yet. What we know and what we can prove are two separate things, you know. Because of all that is involved we must be very, very careful. This can't all be quietly swept under the carpet with a discreet little suicide. The prince and the Home Office want an example made. So do I."

"A trial?"

"And an execution," Sir said, nodding. "But we'll need proof. Your job is to get it."

"It will be done," Anthony promised softly.

"I rather thought you'd say that," Sir answered, folding his arms across his chest. "However, don't be overeager. Grayson is too dangerous to risk your taking him alone. You'll be needing help if my plan is to work."

"That's why you're here, I take it?"

"Only indirectly." Sir was starting to grin, a devil of amusement shining in his bright blue eyes. "But for your associate I had someone else in mind. Someone no one, not even Jonathan, would suspect."

"Not Shipton." The very idea filled Anthony with horror. "If you've no objections, Sir, I should very much like to survive this mission!"

"Not Shipton," Sir agreed in a soothing manner.

"Then who?"

"Why, your Lady X, of course," Sir said, his grin widening at Anthony's expression. "She succeeded in hoodwinking us, didn't she?"

"Well, yes," Anthony agreed with visible reluctance. "But I thought you never used women in your work."

"I don't. But then, Miss Malvern is no ordinary woman."

Anthony couldn't argue with that. In fact, during the past two weeks he had been thinking much the same thing. But still . . . "It's much too dangerous," he decided, running a hand through his hair. "She'd be certain to get herself or someone else killed."

"There is that possibility." Sir was never one to minimize the risks he and his men took as their duty. "But from what you've said, there's no one else in the house we can trust. And it is imperative that we eliminate Grayson as soon as possible."

"I agree, Sir," Anthony protested, feeling somewhat frustrated. "But I have always worked alone. If you insist I take on a partner, then assign me a seasoned agent. Someone who understands the danger!"

"There is no one else," Sir replied bluntly. "The others are already in positions elsewhere, and I don't dare pull them out. Besides, as I have said, this is a matter of the greatest urgency, and we don't have enough time to place another agent in the household without arousing suspicion." He regarded Anthony over his wineglass. "Are you saying Miss Malvern won't help us?"

"Jacinda? My God, she'll probably want to go right up to Jonathan and shoot him!" Anthony exclaimed in disgust. "She's a managing, interfering, rebellious hellcat! I'd spend half my time rescuing her from her own folly, and the other half of the time wondering what new mischief she was plotting. It simply won't work."

"Why, Marchfield, are you saying you can't handle one demure little spinster?"

"Demure? Jacinda?" Anthony shook his head. "You saw her today. Would you call *that* demure?"

"Perhaps not," Sir agreed, pouring more wine into his glass and Anthony's. "But she is a woman. I've seen you work your charms on some of the most sophisticated women in London. Surely one bookish female shouldn't be so difficult for you to control."

Anthony's jaw hardened, and the look he gave Sir fairly dripped with ice. "Are you suggesting that I seduce Miss Malvern into cooperating?" he asked coldly.

"Do you think it would work?" Sir seemed more curious than annoyed with Anthony's display of temper.

"How the devil would I know?" Anthony snapped, his eyes glacial with fury. "But I'm damned well not going to find out!"

"If you don't ask her, I will." Sir raised his glass to his lips. "From what I have seen of her, she is a woman who would be willing to do whatever the situation called for."

"I know she would!" Anthony felt like cursing. "That's just it. Jacinda would be perfect for what you want, but damn it, I don't want her involved! She could be hurt, killed . . ." Anthony's voice broke and he glanced out the window of the carriage, unable to continue.

"I know." Abruptly Sir was serious, the laughter dying from his eyes as he studied Anthony.

"And if there was any other way I could do this, I would. But there's simply no other way."

"Couldn't you help me?" Anthony asked, rubbing a weary hand over his neck. "I know there's always a chance Jonathan would recognize you, even if you were in disguise. But we could try it, couldn't we?"

Sir shook his head. "It's too risky. There's every chance I would be recognized, and then Jonathan is bound to realize he has been found out and bolt. It's a matter of national security that he be taken . . . alive, if possible. Besides, I've already been assigned a role in the coming drama."

Anthony glanced up at Sir's words. "Meaning?" he asked, although he already knew the answer.

"Meaning that I shall be the bait we use to flush out our prey. Listen carefully, Anthony. This is what I want you and your Miss Malvern to do."

Chapter Ten

Jacinda spent the remainder of the afternoon in her study contemplating her future. Anthony's discovery of her true identity showed her the futility of continued secrecy. She knew she could trust him to keep her secret, but she also knew she couldn't endure the suspense another day.

She'd rather confess everything now, and be done with it. And as for his insistence that he would admit to being Lady X to save her reputation . . . there was no way she would allow him to make such a sacrifice. It was time to end the charade.

What did it matter if she was socially ostracized, she argued silently. She was hardly the belle of the ball now, and she had never really enjoyed the endless balls, routs, and soirees that made up society. Once she was out of London she could do as she pleased. The only thing she had to gain by making a clean breast of it was her freedom, and the more she looked at it, the sweeter that freedom seemed.

The only problem she could foresee was what would become of her. It was obvious she couldn't remain with her aunt and uncle, which meant she would be forced to seek a position as a governess or a companion. Much as she disliked the notion she didn't see that she would have any other choice; options for a female in her position were extremely limited. She supposed she could try supporting herself with her writing, but that seemed a precarious living at best.

Another consideration was that she no longer wished to continue writing the *Journals*. Anthony's charge that she had endangered the country with her silly prattling had shaken her. Her intentions might have been harmless, but would that matter if her carelessness had cost men their lives? The very notion horrified her, as did the realization that she had hurt several innocent people's feelings. She more than anyone knew how deeply words could cut, yet she'd never given their sensibilities a moment's consideration.

She'd been so self-righteous, so certain they deserved her smug digs and sly innuendos that she'd forgotten her targets were flesh-and-blood men and women with thoughts and emotions she could never understand. In poking fun at their foibles and weaknesses she'd become as bad as those she vilified in her parodies. It was time to put Lady X to rest, and with that thought in mind, she picked up her quill and composed a letter to her publisher.

After placing the letter to Mr. Fairchild in her uncle's study to be franked and sent on to London, she hurried to her rooms and changed for dinner. The storm that had been threatening all afternoon broke with a vengeance while she was dressing, and listening to the rain beat against the mullioned windows, she donned a paisley shawl over her gown of rose bombazine before joining the others in the dining room.

Following a quiet dinner, they retired to the drawing room for an evening of cards and conversation. Naturally the duke's absence caused a great deal of comment, and Jacinda found herself besieged by questions from the curious guests.

"You might have sent for me, Jacinda," Cassandra rebuked her with a childish pout. "You should have known I would want to wish him a safe journey."

"He was only going to Dover, cousin," Jacinda pointed out, less inclined than usual to cater to the spoiled girl, "not to the ends of the earth.

Besides, as I have told Mr. Blakely, his grace was in something of a hurry."

"Well, I hope he is in an equal hurry to return. This is no night to be out on the cliff road," Lady Shipton said, casting an uneasy glance at the windows. Even though the drapes had been drawn against the storm, flashes of lightning could still be seen, and the wind whistled about the brick house like a wild thing. "When did his grace say he would return?"

"He didn't, ma'am," Jacinda answered, sharing her aunt's concern for Anthony's safety. The cliff road was treacherous on the best of nights, and on a night such as this it could be deadly. Mudslides weren't all that uncommon following a storm, nor was it unheard of for a coach to be swept from the cliff by fierce winds. Her eyes strayed to the window, her hands clenching on her lap as she sent up a silent prayer.

"Well, at least this weather should keep the gentlemen in," Peter remarked, helping himself to a second glass of sherry. He was dressed in an evening coat of dark red velvet that clashed with the brilliant copper of his thick hair. "You did say that they were thick as fleas hereabouts, didn't you, my lord?" He addressed the question to the earl, who was already deep into his third glass of brandy.

"Eh?" Lord Shipton glanced up, blinking sleepily at Peter. "Or . . . er . . . quite. Only I didn't call the rascals 'gentlemen.' Smugglers they are, and smugglers I shall name them. The ruffians are a menace to us all."

"But a necessary menace, don't you think?"

Peter drawled languidly, his bright blue eyes resting on the earl. "Were it not for them, whatever would good honest Englishmen do for brandy? Not to mention what our lovely ladies would do for silks and satins."

The earl set his snifter down with a loud thump, his face purpling with rage. Jacinda sensed they were about to be subjected to one of his long-winded tirades, and hoping to save both the company and herself from a potential scene, she turned to Peter with a bright smile.

"It is interesting you should mention smugglers, Mr. Blakely," she said, casting him a speaking glance. "I was reading a book only last week by one of the Roman historians. It seems smugglers and pirates were also quite a problem in Hadrian's day. Isn't that fascinating?"

"If you say so, Miss Malvern." He acquiesced to her change of subject with a sardonic smile. "Although I fear I must take your word for it. I have never read the works of any historian, Roman or otherwise, and I have no intention of doing so. As a wit, I make it a habit never to be overly informed on any subject." He took another drink of his wine before sending her an innocent look.

"Your devotion to such things, however, seems only natural," he continued. "You are, after all, an acknowledged bluestocking. With your great love of books I wonder that you never gave any thought to becoming a writer."

"Thank you, Mr. Blakely," she replied, her cheeks paling with alarm. She would never have a better opportunity than now to confess, she realized, nervously pleating the fabric of her gown. Because the ball was being held tomorrow night, many of the guests had already retired to their rooms. With the exception of the marquess, Lord Jonathan, Mr. Vale, and Peter, the only other persons present were members of her family.

The idea of making her announcement in front of the guests made her tongue-tied with horror, but if she must, she would manage somehow. If only Anthony were here, she thought wistfully. She felt she could dare anything in his comforting presence. But without him here she longed to make a strategic retreat, an event made all the more desirable by Peter's next words.

"You are most welcome, Miss Malvern," Peter responded in his drawling voice. "But really, I am serious, you know. With your intellectual abilities, I'm sure you would go far."

Jacinda's eyes flew to his, and in their mocking blue depths she read the truth; he knew. The very thing she feared most was upon her, and there was nothing she could do but face her fate with as much courage as she could muster. She raised her chin, meeting his eyes with firm resolve.

"As a matter of fact, Mr. Blakely, the thought has crossed my mind," she said coolly. "What would you recommend I try? A play, perhaps? A novel? *Journals?*" She flung the word at him like a gauntlet.

"*Journals?*" Mr. Vale said, he and the marquess glancing up in surprise. "Is he still harping on those silly *Journals?*" Daniel asked, leaving the whist table to settle beside Jacinda. "Don't let him plague you anymore, ma'am, for I have already solved the riddle of Lady X."

Jacinda's stomach dropped to her toes, but she clung determinedly to her pride. She drew her shoulders back and faced Daniel. "Indeed, Mr. Vale? And pray, who do you think Lady X might be?"

"Please, don't encourage the fellow, Miss Malvern," Peter drawled, flicking his lace cuffs over his wrists as he shot Daniel a superior smile. "You must know, dear boy, that your charge that our very own Wilmount is Lady X is utter moonshine! Willie is the most exemplary of hosts, but to think him capable of writing the *Journals* . . . well, that is expecting rather a bit much of the fellow, don't you think?"

Lady Shipton's brows snapped together at this two-pronged attack on her beloved son. While the earl and Wilmount indignantly defended themselves, she entered into the fray with the fierceness of a lioness defending her cub. For a moment it was uncertain which attack she would first counter, but in the end her furious gaze fell on Peter.

"The viscount," she stressed her son's title with imperious scorn, "was at the top of his form in both literature and the arts. And as I once remarked to the Duke of Marchfield, literary excellence is a family tradition. Where do you think Jacinda inherited her interest?"

"Then you openly admit your son is Lady X?" the marquess demanded, drawing his skeletal frame erect. "Well! This is a fine way to treat one's guests, I must say!"

Lady Shipton rounded on him with all guns blazing. "My Wilmount is most assuredly not that common gossip monger!" she snapped, her jowls quaking in fury. "I was merely pointing out to Mr. Blakely that if Wilmount wanted to write them, he could have easily done so! But if you want *my* opinion, Lady X is in this room, and I am looking right at him!" Her blazing dark eyes settled on a smirking Peter.

"If you mean me, my lady, I fear I must disappoint you," Peter replied languidly, oblivious to the hostile glances being cast his way by the others. "Besides, the bet was my idea, remember? I would scarcely have done such a thing if I were indeed Lady X."

"A clever ruse," Willie said, shuffling forward to glare at his friend with marked suspicion. "But *I* saw through it at once! You always did have a devilish cutting tongue, Blakely. Don't know why I didn't tumble to it before."

Jacinda drew a deep breath as she reached for the courage to end this farcical scene. She had no idea why Peter hadn't denounced her, but she knew she couldn't sit idly by and let an innocent man be accused of her crime. She wet her lips with a nervous tongue, her heart hammering in her throat as she said, "Aunt, Uncle, there is something I need to tell—"

"By gad, Wilmount, you are right!" Daniel interrupted, leaping to his feet, his dark eyes wide with incredulity as he studied Peter's face. "Why, at Eaton you were forever writing those scurrilous letters to the dean . . . Remember, Wilmount? And you wrote all our billets-doux for us now that I think of it!" He shook his head in wonder, a slow smile warming his usually solemn features. "Peter, I vow, you are the most complete hand!"

"No, you mustn't accuse Mr. Blakely," Jacinda insisted, determined now to make her confession. "He is innocent! He isn't Lady X, I—"

"Oh, Jacinda, hush!" Lady Shipton cried, sinking into her chair and groping for her smelling salts. "We have enough on our plates just now without listening to your nonsense. I swear the shame of this will surely carry me off." She cast Peter a fulminating glare that belied her supposedly delicate condition. "I might have known it was you," she muttered darkly. "Any man who would wear that shade of red is not to be trusted, I have always thought so."

"But, Aunt Prudence, you must listen—"

"My congratulations, Mr. Blakely." Lord Jonathan bowed to Peter, his brown eyes merry with amusement. "And might I say how much I have enjoyed your work? Your sense of wordplay is masterful, I assure you."

"But he's not—"

"You might have given me more mention in your *Journals,* Mr. Blakely," Cassandra pouted, fluttering her lashes at Peter. "You gave that awful Sally Grantfield two whole pages in your last work, and I'm much more prominent than she is!"

"Must be a Whig," Lord Shipton volunteered to no one in particular. "It sounds like one of their tricks. I don't know what the prince will have to say about this, although he likes the *Journals.* Keeps 'em by his bed."

"The scandal, the scandal," the countess moaned, clutching a hand to her bosom. "They will say we were a part of it, and then where shall we be?"

"Will someone please listen to me!" Jacinda leapt to her feet, golden fires sparkling in her hazel eyes. "I'm telling you, Mr. Blakely is *not* Lady X! I—"

"Save your breath, Miss Jacinda," Peter said; his lips twisting in a wry grin as he met her earnest gaze. "For in a way they're right, you know. Had I thought of it first, I *would* have been Lady X."

"Aha! I knew I was right!" the marquess gloated, jabbing his finger at Peter. "He even admits his guilt!"

"There, you see, ma'am? Tried and condemned without a shred of evidence." Peter sighed dramatically. "But my thanks for your spirited defense, Miss Jacinda, for all the good it did. You can see they will not believe you."

"But—"

"No, no more, I pray you. Your protestations are quite useless, and really, they are becoming a bore." He covered an indifferent yawn with a well-shaped hand. "Next I suppose you will be claiming that you are Lady X."

A loud chorus of derisive laughter greeted his taunt, and Lady Shipton spoke sharply before Jacinda could open her mouth. "Don't be ridiculous, child! If you don't have anything sensible to contribute to the conversation, then kindly leave."

Jacinda's mouth slammed shut. Fine, she thought with mounting anger. She tried doing the honorable thing, and where did it get her? If they didn't want to hear her confession, she certainly wasn't going to force it upon them! She lifted her head proudly as she faced her aunt.

"Very well, my lady," she said in a stiff voice. "If that is your wish, I will retire. Uncle, cousin, I bid you good night."

"One moment, Miss Jacinda, I believe I shall also seek my bed," Peter said, rising quickly to his feet. "I find all this accusation business exhausting!"

"But you can't leave now!" Wilmount protested indignantly. "What about the *Journals*?"

"What about the miserable things?" Peter wanted to know. "You claim I wrote them, I insist I have not. I fail to see what we have left to discuss."

"But what about the bet?" Mr. Vale exclaimed. "It still stands, doesn't it? And if you and Miss Jacinda aren't Lady X, then who is?"

"That I will leave to the rest of you," Peter answered with haughty indifference. "As for me, I am sorry I even brought the matter up; it has grown tiresome. Until tomorrow, then." And he escorted Jacinda from the room, ignoring their vociferous objections.

Out in the hall Jacinda turned to face him. "And what was all that about?" she wanted to know. "Why didn't you say something?"

He arched his copper-colored eyebrows in horror. "What? And ruin all the fun? Come, Miss Jacinda, you can't be so lacking in imagination as all that!" He gave her a cheeky grin. "I'll wager a monkey that before this weekend is over the only person who won't be charged with being Lady X is the good duke. Think of the possible accusations, the heated denials, the woeful recriminations . . . you wouldn't be so cruel as to deny me my small pleasures, would you?"

She shook her head at his boyish enthusiasm. "I fear Mr. Vale is right, Mr. Blakely. You are the most complete hand! And a dedicated mischief maker," she added with a rueful laugh.

"So I am, ma'am, so I am." He dipped his head in acknowledgment. "But let's make that our little secret, shall we?" One blue eye closed in a teasing wink. "What's one more little secret between friends, hmm? Good night, Miss Jacinda. Sleep well."

It was approaching midnight before an exhausted Anthony returned to the Hall. The journey back from Dover had been long and dangerous, and there were times he regretted setting out for Folkstone instead of waiting out the storm as the coachman suggested. But Sir had made it obvious that matters were rapidly approaching the crisis point, and the sooner Grayson was captured, the better for all.

He found most of the guests were abed when he entered the drawing room, and when he inquired after Jacinda he was informed she had already retired for the evening.

"Is there anything I can do to help you, Your

Grace?" his hostess volunteered with a hopeful smile. "You've missed your dinner, and I'm sure you must be famished. I can have the cook prepare a cold collation, if you'd like."

"No, I'm fine, my lady, thank you," Anthony replied politely. "If you will pardon me, I believe I shall go up to my rooms. I am rather tired."

His valet was waiting in his rooms, and after a moment's consideration Anthony dashed off a letter to Jacinda. The proprieties be damned, he decided, handing the note to John; this couldn't wait until morning.

"Take this to Miss Malvern's room," he instructed in the crisp tone his servant had been trained not to question. "Tell her it is extremely important that I speak with her tonight, and then bring her back here."

"To your rooms, Your Grace?" Training or no, the request brought the valet's eyebrows up in astonishment.

"To my rooms," Anthony repeated, the ice in his gray eyes daring the man to object again. "And need I say it is imperative for the lady's reputation that you not be seen?"

"Of course, Your Grace." John bristled at the very suggestion that he should be so lax in his duties. "Will there be anything else?"

"No, just see to it that we're not disturbed."

"As you wish, sir." He gave a stiff bow and then left the room.

In his absence Anthony removed his jacket and loosened his cravat. He supposed for appearance's sake it would be better for him to remain fully clothed, but the truth of it was he was exhausted, and he couldn't endure the rigid confines of the tight jacket another moment. Besides, he thought, his mouth tilting in a soft smile, Jacinda wasn't the sort of female who would swoon at the sight of a man in his shirtsleeves.

He crossed the sitting room to the cellarette, and poured himself a glass of brandy. The rain was still falling, lashed into a stinging fury by the strong winds, and he could hear it striking the panes of glass in the tall window. At least it had stopped lightning, he thought, raising the snifter to his lips. He would rather face a regiment of French dragoons than be out in the open on such a night.

He rested his broad shoulder against the oak mantel of the fireplace, staring down into the dying flames of the fire. Sir's plan had much to recommend it, he admitted silently, and despite his initial resistance to the idea, he knew there was really no other choice. If they hoped to trap Grayson, Jacinda's cooperation was essential; it was that simple. He couldn't allow his personal feelings to cloud his judgment. No matter what, he had to win her support.

"Anthony? You wanted to see me?" His head came up at the soft words, and he turned to find Jacinda hovering in the doorway, an uncertain smile on her face.

She was dressed in a warm night robe of loden green, her light brown hair falling down her back in a thick plait. Realizing that she looked as awkward as he felt, he hastened to set her at her ease.

"Thank you for coming so quickly," he said, moving forward to take her hand in his. "You must know it was vital or I would never have asked you here," he added, assisting her into the large overstuffed chair in front of the fireplace.

"I know," she replied, her eyes wide as she studied his handsome face in the flickering red glow of the fire. "Is this about that poor prisoner?" she asked, her heart pounding as the silence between them grew heavy. "Did he . . . did he die?"

"Unhappily, yes," Anthony answered, remembering the emaciated man he and Sir had visited in the prison hospital. Sir, in his usual, efficient way, had made sure there would be verification of his story should anyone check. There was even a Brother Peter who tended the prisoners' needs.

Anthony's expression grew bleak as he recalled the officer's faltering voice as he spoke of his wife and infant son, and the tender good-byes he had sent them. The letter was now tucked safely in Sir's pocket, and he knew that come what may, it would be delivered into the wife's hands. Sir had given the man his word.

"I'm sorry," Jacinda whispered, noting the grim look in Anthony's light gray eyes. Without considering their unorthodox situation she took his cold hand in hers, cradling it against her cheek. "Forgive me for scolding you in the kitchen," she said softly. "I know you're not the type of man to shirk his reponsibilities."

"You're too generous, ma'am," he replied in a husky voice, brushing his finger across her full lips. "But you shouldn't feel guilty for your actions. They were most helpful, I assure you. Certainly Sir seemed to think so."

"Sir?" Her brow puckered at the name.

"Yes, he was most impressed at the way you dressed me down," he continued in a teasing vein, carefully extracting his hand from hers and moving away. He was too aware of the lateness of the hour and the soft darkness surrounding them to trust his good intentions.

"I wasn't dressing you down! I was merely reminding you of your duty, and—" She stopped abruptly as the significance of his words hit her. "Sir?" she gasped. "You've seen him? When?"

"This afternoon." He grinned at her incredulous expression. "He blessed you, in fact."

"That was Sir?"

"Yes, but don't be disappointed that you didn't suspect anything. He's even fooled me a time or two."

"Yes, but I should have at least guessed," she grumbled, chagrined at how easily she had been deceived. "I mean, a *monk,* for heaven's sake! I should have known something was amiss the moment I set eyes on him, but I was so angry when you refused to help that poor man that I . . . There was a prisoner, wasn't there?" She surveyed him suspiciously.

"There was. There's even a Brother Peter should anyone ask. Sir never leaves anything to chance."

"And to think I missed him. I don't suppose he'll be coming back?" she asked, cocking her head at him inquiringly.

"Actually, we did discuss it," he admitted, aware his hand was beginning to shake with emotion. The small sign of his agitation shocked him, and he willed himself to continue. "Jacinda, do you remember I once told you that Sir never used women as agents?"

"Yes," she answered slowly, aware of his mounting tension.

"Something has come up . . . a matter of the greatest urgency that makes it necessary for him . . . for us to violate that directive. If there was any other way I—" His voice broke off as he thrust an impatient hand through his hair. "Blast it all, Jacinda!" he growled, meeting her astonished gaze. "We need your help!"

Her heart leapt at his impassioned words. "What is it you want?"

Anthony helped himself to another glass of brandy before facing her again. "There's a traitor in our ranks," he said curtly. "He has already betrayed several of our men into enemy hands, and we believe he's plotting to assassinate Sir. We have an idea . . . a trap to catch him. But in order to spring it we'll need your help.

"It's dangerous," he continued, even though she made no attempt to speak. "I won't lie to you, Jacinda. You could be hurt, perhaps even killed. This man is as ruthless as he is cunning, and it won't be easy deceiving him."

"I understand, Anthony," she said gently, her eyes resting on his face. A lock of dark hair had fallen across his forehead, and her fingers trembled with the urge to brush it back. "Do you know the traitor's name?"

"It's Grayson."

"Lord Jonathan!" Jacinda gasped in dismay, unwilling to believe the affable young man could be guilty of so heinous a crime. "Are you certain?"

"Yes." Anthony rubbed the back of his neck in a tired gesture. "There's absolutely no doubt that he's a double agent who has been selling us out to the French."

Her heart went out to Anthony at the harsh lines etched deeply in his face. It was obvious his colleague's treason affected him deeply, and she longed to comfort him. But before she could act on her impulse he said, "Sir and I agree that he is the one who stole the *Journals* from my room. That he hasn't denounced you is proof of that. He's probably holding on to the *Journals* to see what I will do. That's where you come in."

"Do I get to steal them back?" She brightened, wondering if she should tell him about the debacle in the drawing room. She was certain he would be amused.

"Lord, no!" He winced at her words and the eager sparkle in her eyes. "If that's all there was to it, I could do it all myself."

"Spoilsport," she accused with a pout. "You're selfish, Anthony, to want to hog all the fun to yourself, and after tonight I should think you would want to get the *Journals* under lock and key."

"Why? What happened?" he asked warily.

She told him in a few pithy sentences, and as she suspected, a reluctant smile softened his features as she described Peter's reasons for keeping her identity secret.

"Thank God Blakely was able to keep you from confessing," he said, his eyes glowing with amusement at her telling descriptions. "It would have ruined everything if you had blurted everything out in front of Grayson."

"Why?" She frowned in confusion. "He must know who I am. He has the *Journals,* after all."

"Yes, but he doesn't know that *you* are aware of that fact," Anthony explained patiently. "As far as he's concerned I still suspect you as a French spy, and—" He broke off, his head snapping toward the door.

"Anthony, what—"

"Shh!" He silenced her with a wave of his hand. "I thought I heard something." He pulled the knife from his sleeve, approaching the door without making a sound. When he reached the door, he paused, laying his ear against the smooth wood as he strained to catch any noise. After several seconds had passed he relaxed his shoulders.

"Nothing," he said, swinging back to face her. "It must have been mice I heard."

"Or the storm. It's blowing something terrible out there," she reminded him.

"I know, I was out in the thick of it. Now, where was I?" He returned to his post before the fire.

"You were saying that Lord Jonathan still thinks you suspect me of being a spy."

"Yes, and you are to enforce that notion by going to him and asking him for his help. Tell him I have discovered you're Lady X and am threatening to have you arrested."

"What?" She straightened in her chair. "But why should I do that? If he's a traitor—"

"He *is* a traitor; you must never doubt that,

Jacinda." Anthony spoke with a deadly seriousness that made Jacinda shiver with dread. "As I said, Grayson is ruthless, and he'd kill you without a moment's hesitation if he even suspected you of helping us. Do you understand?"

"Yes," she said, meeting his gaze bravely. "And I'll be careful, Anthony, I promise you. But won't he think it strange that I come to him? How am I to know if he is a spy, or whatever it is you and Sir call yourselves?"

"Let him discover you . . . preferably in tears, and you can blurt everything out in an emotional display," Anthony instructed, thinking the plan didn't sound nearly as foolproof now as when Sir first proposed it. If Grayson even suspected Jacinda . . . He refused to consider the consequences.

"I suppose I could do that." She laid a finger on her lip as she considered his words. "But I still think he'll be suspicious. After all, you've had the *Journals* for weeks. That is, he's had them, but it's all very much the same thing, isn't it? If you know I'm Lady X, then why have you waited until now to arrest me? It doesn't make sense!"

"That's because you don't know how Sir operates," he replied, growing weary of standing and easing himself onto the chair beside hers. "But Grayson does. He'll know I wouldn't be able to make a move until I had contacted Sir about you . . . which I did, as a matter of fact."

"What did he say?" She was intrigued by his confession.

"He agrees with me." Anthony gave her a tender smile. "You might be a menace, Jacinda, but it has been decided that you are a harmless menace. However, that's not what you're to tell Grayson."

"You're to be painted as the blackest of villains, I take it?" she quizzed, her eyes dancing with laughter. "Hmm, something tells me I shall enjoy this spy business."

"Just don't get carried away in your role as a damsel in distress," he cautioned. "Grayson hasn't survived this long by being a fool, and if you overplay things he's bound to smell a trap."

"I'll be discretion itself," she promised, beginning to grow excited at the prospect of helping to catch a spy. "I'll wait until after the ball, and then I'll—"

"We can't wait that long," Anthony interrupted reluctantly. "I know it's tomorrow night, but if possible we hope to have him in irons by then."

"How?"

"When you tell him I'm threatening to have you carted away, you'll also tell him I have been contacted by my superior and am acting under his direct orders. Grayson is smart enough to realize that Sir was here disguised as Brother Peter, and that he is probably in Dover."

"But what will that prove?" she asked, puzzled by the intricacies of the scheme.

"Nothing, until he goes to Dover and tries to kill Sir," Anthony answered without bothering to wrap the bald facts up in pretty linen. Perhaps if Jacinda understood the deadly consequences of failure she would cease looking upon this as some sort of grand adventure . . . which he strongly suspected was the case.

"But that's terrible!" she cried, her hand fluttering up to her throat. "What if he succeeds?"

"He won't," he promised her with grim resolve. "But the fact that he even makes the attempt will seal his fate. He will hang." Again he used the most brutal images he could think of, determined to impress the dangers of the situation on Jacinda's mind.

"Well, it's no less than he deserves." Her fierce tone surprised him. "The man's a traitor, after all. Very well, if it can't wait then I'll arrange to meet him tomorrow while he's out riding. He likes to ride near the cliffs, you know. Or into the village."

"I know," Anthony answered quietly, wishing that there was some other way, any other way to trap Grayson. The thought of Jacinda out on the high cliffs with a man who had proven himself a merciless killer made him quake with fear. He wanted to send her someplace far away until the danger was past, and for some odd reason the first place he thought of was his own estate in Devonshire.

A secret smile softened his lips at the image of her roaming up and down the corridors of his ancestral home. His mother kept a study in the back of the house near the gardens; she could write her books there, and in the afternoons they could ride about the grounds together. He could almost see her light brown hair blowing behind her like a silken banner, her eyes bright with laughter as she took a fence . . .

"Well, now that that's decided, I think I'll return to my rooms," Jacinda said in a brisk tone. She noted the thoughtful expression on Anthony's face, and decided it meant he wanted to be alone. "Shall I let you know when I've spoken with him?"

"That's a good idea," he approved, impatient with himself for his silly daydreaming. "Send a message through John. We're probably being watched too closely to risk another meeting."

"Very well." Jacinda rose to her feet. She was surprised by the emotions plaguing her, including the shameful desire that made her wish Anthony would take her in his arms and never let her go. "I'll bid you good night, then." Without waiting for him to see her out she hurried to the door, twisting the knob in her eagerness to be gone. It refused to move.

"What on earth?" She tried again, but to no avail.

"What is it?" He walked up behind her.

"It's the door," she said, pushing on it with her shoulder. "It's stuck."

"Here, let me try." He pushed her gently aside, throwing his considerable weight against the door as he pulled on the knob. He tried several times, his shoulders hitting the door with great force, but it refused to open. Finally he leaned against it, closing his eyes as he realized what the sound he had heard must have been—a key turning in a lock.

"What is it, Anthony?" Jacinda asked, biting her lip as she met his fierce gaze. "What's wrong with the door? I can't imagine how it might have become stuck. We've never had any trouble with it before."

"It's not stuck, Jacinda," he said in a quiet voice, straightening his shoulders as he rose to his full height. "It's been locked. And you, my dear, have been locked in here with me. For the night, it would seem."

Chapter Eleven

"Locked in?" Jacinda gasped, staring at Anthony in dismay as the meaning of his words sank in. "Are you certain?"

"Positive," he replied, giving the doorknob a final rattle. "We've been caught as neatly as two rats in a trap. Blast!" He slammed his fist against the solid wood. "I should have known something like this would happen!"

Jacinda flinched at his vehemence. She was only too aware of the implications should they be found together, and she didn't relish the thought of discovery any more than he did. With that thought in mind she approached the door with renewed determination. "This is an old house, and the doors often stick. Aunt is forever complaining about it," she said, placing her hand against the wood as if testing its resilience. "Perhaps if we were to push against it at the same time we could force it open."

Anthony doubted it would do much good, but at this point he was willing to try anything. They spent the next several minutes flinging their combined weight against the thick wood in an effort to break the lock. "It's no use, Jacinda," he said at last, his breathing ragged from his exertions. "The door has been locked and the key taken away."

Jacinda retreated to her chair before the fireplace, rubbing her aching shoulder distractedly. "But who would do such a thing?" she asked, studying him with wide eyes. "And why? What could they hope to gain?"

"My guess would be Grayson," he replied, crossing to stand in front of the fireplace. "He undoubtedly hopes to discredit me and any charges I make against him. Or perhaps he means to make an escape while I'm locked in here. I have no idea, and in the end it really doesn't signify. What does matter," he said, drawing himself up and meeting her gaze unflinchingly, "is that we have been compromised, and we have no other course open to us except marriage."

"Marriage!" she exclaimed, gaping at him as if he had taken leave of his senses. She knew the situation was serious, but for him to propose marriage in so cold and forthright a manner had her head spinning in shock.

"Of course, marriage!" he replied, frowning at the stunned look on her face. "My word, Jacinda, what kind of man do you take me for? It's my fault your reputation has been ruined. Naturally I shall do the honorable thing."

"Well, thank you very much, Your Grace!" she

bristled defensively. "The proposal every girl dreams of, I am sure!"

Anthony uttered a strangled oath at her willfulness. He might have known she would dig in her heels at the very notion of behaving in anything approaching a sensible manner. Did she honestly think they could dance out of here in the morning with no recriminations whatsoever? Well, he decided, his jaw hardening with resolve, she wasn't the only one involved here. If she didn't care if her name was dragged through the mud of scandal, he did.

"If this isn't the proposal you have longed for, Miss Malvern, then neither is it the way I imagined myself making an offer," he informed her, determined that she should behave in a rational manner. "I hadn't thought to marry for a good many years yet, and I certainly never envisioned that I should be forced to do so to avoid a scandal. But there is nothing else to be done. We're getting married, Jacinda, and that's the end of it."

"Oh, is it indeed, Your Grace?" she shot back, blinking back the angry tears that scalded her eyes. Anthony's words cut her to the marrow, and in that moment she realized the full measure of her folly. She loved Anthony, loved him more than she dreamed could be possible, and she'd be hanged if she would allow his rigid sense of honor and duty to force him into a marriage he so obviously found repellent.

"Yes, by God, it is," he returned with all the haughtiness at his command. Much to his surprise the idea of marriage to Jacinda was growing increasingly attractive, and he was resolved she

would do as he ordered. After all, he would have
to marry eventually, and it might as well be
Jacinda as some other chit. She was intelligent,
attractive, and if her birth didn't equal his it was
still respectable. At least he'd never be bored, he
thought with a sudden flash of whimsy. He had a
feeling she would keep him on his toes for the
rest of their lives.

"Well, perhaps you have no objections to being
forced down the aisle, but I am no Bath miss to
be led meekly where I would not go!" Jacinda
retorted, refusing for even one moment to consider his sullen proposal. Such a marriage would
be a travesty of what she yearned for with him,
and in the end she knew he could only come to
resent her.

"Hang it all, Jacinda, can't you see there is no
other choice?" he shouted, maddened by her obstreperous refusal to accept his offer. "We have
been compromised! It is my duty to marry you,
and by God, I shall marry you, with or without
your cooperation!"

"How very noble of you, Your Grace, but before you fling yourself on the sacrificial altar,
might I suggest we try one other thing?"

"What?" He scowled at her sharp words.

"Ring for the valet and have him bring the
key."

His eyes flew from her face to the paisley rope
pull hanging discreetly in the corner. He felt his
face flood with color as he realized, much to his
chagrin, that such a simple solution hadn't even
occurred to him. For someone trained to think in

a cool and rational fashion regardless of the situation, this was a lowering thought.

"That will never do," he said, hiding his embarrassment behind a gruff manner. "John will have retired by now, and besides, where would he get another key?"

"From the housekeeper, of course," she said, baring her teeth in a mock smile. "She keeps several sets in the pantry; he has only to ask and one will be found."

He frowned at that, turning her suggestion over in his mind before rejecting it. "No, that still doesn't answer. Even if he does find a key and manages to open the door, you'll still be found in my rooms and wearing your nightclothes. The only difference is you should be discovered now rather than later, and I hardly think that would solve our problem."

"I'll hide," Jacinda suggested, hanging on to her resolve with tenuous control. The thought of marriage to Anthony was almost irresistibly sweet, and she feared her ability to hold out much longer.

"Oh, yes, and a fine French farce that would make when you are found cowering in the wardrobe!"

"Then I'll tie the bedclothes together and go out the window!" she cried in desperation, leaping to her feet and facing him across the dimly lit sitting room. "I mean it, Anthony," she added when he stared at her in mute disbelief. "Either you ring for your valet and have him fetch the key or I'll go out the window, and there's nothing you can do to stop me."

For a moment Anthony was speechless. He had been so conditioned to think of himself as the ultimate matrimonial prize that it never occurred to him his suit would be rejected. The realization that she was so vehemently opposed to marrying him that she would risk life and limb to avoid such a fate was oddly hurtful, and for a moment part of him wanted to lash out in rage. But then in the next minute his pride came to his rescue. If she didn't wish to marry him, fine.

"Very well, Miss Malvern," he said in a voice as icy as the shimmer in his eyes. "If that is how you feel, I will ring for John. But might I suggest that you keep hidden until the door has been opened? Whoever locked us in may still be about, and we may yet find ourselves explaining things to your uncle."

In the end opening the door proved absurdly simple. The valet, trained by years of service with the duke, didn't even turn a hair at finding him locked in his room with Jacinda. Once a duplicate key had been found he had the door opened in a trice, and less than ten minutes later Jacinda was safely tucked back in her bed.

Lying in the darkness, she found her thoughts returning again and again to Anthony's proposal. Should she have accepted? she wondered, staring up at the canopy of her bed with burning eyes. He seemed sincere in his offer, and she knew instinctively that he would make an excellent husband. He was a man of honor, and at least she would never need fear that he would betray his marriage vows. He may not love her, but she knew him well enough to know he would never hurt her by seeking other women.

And children, she dreamed, her heart constricting with pain. He would be a good and loving father to their children. She'd never given children much thought, but now she could almost see them. A black-haired son, with the same solemn air as his father, and the same lock of hair that fell across his forehead. And a daughter, she thought, brushing the tears from her eyes; a sweet-smelling cherub with Anthony's rare smile and his light-colored eyes.

She turned her face into the pillow, muffling her sobs in the downy softness. Her dreams were just that . . . dreams, and she would only be hurt if she allowed herself to dwell on them. Anthony had proposed to her not out of love, but out of obligation, and she had done the only thing her heart and pride would allow. The choice had been made, and somehow she would have to live with it. Jacinda clung to that thought as she drifted into a restless sleep filled with the children and happiness she would never know.

Because the ball was to be held that night, the house was all at sixes and sevens when she stumbled down to the breakfast table. She learned from the footman that Anthony was still abed, but that Lord Jonathan and some of the others had risen and were out for a gallop. Hearing Jonathan's name made her remember her promise to help Anthony. Despite the fact that they'd parted so acrimoniously the night before, she was still determined to help him. It was her duty, she told herself doggedly, and if a Marchfield knew his duty, then so did a Malvern.

After finishing a hasty breakfast she went up to her room and changed into her riding habit before going out to the stables in search of the others. Lady Jane had recovered from her inflamed fetlock, and Chelms was more than happy to saddle the pretty mare for her.

"Will you be a'joining the gentlemen, Miss Jacinda?" he asked, assisting her onto the horse's back.

"Are they all together?" she queried, settling herself more firmly in the saddle. For their plan to succeed it would be better if she could catch Lord Jonathan alone, but if need be she supposed she could speak to him with the others present. She could always manage to get him off to one side for a private cozen.

"I don't think so, miss," Chelms answered, scratching his bewhiskered chin thoughtfully. "The viscount and Lord Aimsford said as how they meant to ride into the village, but Lord Jonathan said something about riding out toward the cliff to look at the sea."

"Yes, it's always spectacular after a storm, isn't it?" she agreed, keeping her voice cool as she wrapped the reins around her hand. "Perhaps I shall ride out for a look as well. Thank you, Chelms."

She spent the brief ride to the cliffs plotting her strategy. If Lord Jonathan was half as clever as Anthony said he was, then she would have to weigh her every word with the greatest care.

Tears might work with some men, but she had the impression they would prove ineffectual against a man who had cold-bloodedly betrayed his fellow agents. She was trying to decide how best to approach him when she caught sight of him scrambling up the narrow path that led from the cliff to the beach. When he saw her watching him, he froze, then slowly waved his hand at her.

"Good morning, Miss Malvern, and how are you this fine morning?" he greeted her as she rode over to join him.

"I am well, sir," she replied, her tone cautious. If tears were out, then perhaps some other emotion would answer just as well. Thinking quickly, she gave a bitter laugh. "That is to say, I am as well as can be expected considering I have just been accused of being a traitor!"

"I beg your pardon?" he asked, his brown eyes opening wide in astonishment. "What did you say?"

She bit her lip, her eyes flashing with outrage as she said, "You must forgive me, Lord Jonathan, I am not quite myself this morning. But that man's audacity has me so furious I vow I cannot even think straight!"

"No, please don't apologize," he assured her, moving forward to help her dismount. "You are obviously quite upset and perhaps there is something I can do to be of assistance. What man are you talking about? Who has accused you of treason?"

"The Duke of Marchfield," she said, infusing as much anger as she could into her voice. "He has taken it into his head that I am a French spy who has been slipping secret information to the enemy!"

"Good Lord! Whatever gave him that idea?" His look of confusion was almost perfect, but Jacinda thought she could detect a small gleam of cold intelligence in the velvet depths of his eyes.

She glanced away from him, twisting her riding crop in her hands. "Have I your word . . . as a gentleman, that you will never reveal what I am about to tell you?" she asked, shooting him a speculative look from beneath her lashes.

"Of course, Miss Malvern, you may depend upon me."

"I am Lady X."

"What?"

"I never meant any harm," she entreated earnestly, turning to face him. "It was meant to be a lark, nothing more, I swear it! But the duke says that doesn't matter; he said I compromised our country's security and that I must pay! He's even threatening to have me arrested."

"My word, this does sound serious," he said, whistling softly. "As we are at war an accusation of treason is no laughing matter. But I still don't understand why his grace should think you a spy merely because you wrote some scandalous journals."

"They aren't scandalous!" she defended her work indignantly. "They're only mirrors of what society is truly like, and it's hardly any fault of mine if the ton chooses to conduct themselves in so reprehensible a manner! But that's neither here nor there, I suppose." She sighed, and proceeded to detail Anthony's charges, adding the information on how the confiscated *Journals* had disappeared from his room.

"Naturally, he blamed me," she said, gazing out to sea with her lips set in an angry line. "As if I would be foolish enough to do such a thing!"

"Is that when he threatened to have you arrested?"

"Yes, but he said he would have to speak to his superior before doing anything."

She noted the slight stiffening in his shoulders. "Yes, I can see that he would need some sort of authority before accusing a lady of treason," he agreed, watching her through narrowed eyes. "Has he heard anything, do you know?"

"Oh, indeed he has!" she said with another laugh. "He told me last night that he had just spoken to his superior and that I was to be taken in for questioning. If I'm found to be innocent I will be let go. If not . . ." She shrugged her shoulders.

"But he was in Dover last night, wasn't he?" Lord Jonathan asked, his voice sharp with interest. "Didn't you say he'd gone off with a monk?"

"That's what I thought, but apparently I was mistaken as to the good father's identity!" She ducked her head, waiting a few seconds before adding hesitantly, "There's more."

"More?"

"Yes." She blushed with pretty embarrassment and proceeded to tell him about the scene in Anthony's room, embellishing his fury at finding the door locked.

"I thought for a moment he was going to strike me!" she said, rubbing her arms with her hands. "He kept insisting that I had done it to compromise him, thus forcing him into marrying me . . . as if I would want to be shackled to a beast like him! Thank heavens his valet arrived with another key; otherwise I shudder to think what might have happened."

"I can see why he should think that," he said in a thoughtful tone. "After all, if he were found with you under such circumstances his very honor would be compromised. His charges against you would never be believed, and in any case a gentleman can hardly accuse his wife of treason." He studied her sharply. "Your forgiveness, Miss Malvern, but are you quite certain you didn't lock the door behind you?"

"Lord Jonathan!" she cried in outrage. "How can you accuse me of anything so . . . so devious? And I told you, the duke is a beast as far as I am concerned, and I would as lief be transported as to be forced into marriage with him!"

"Then who did it?"

"How am I to know?" The pout she gave was a perfect imitation of Cassandra at her worst. "Willie, undoubtedly, or Mr. Blakely. It sounds like something they would do. But that doesn't signify. The point remains that I have been charged with betraying my country, and there is nothing I can do about it. What . . . what do you think will become of me?" She allowed a faint tremor to creep into her voice as she regarded him anxiously.

He pretended to consider her statement. "My brother is not without influence," he said at last. "And he is an intimate of the prince's. I'm sure if I asked he could intervene on your behalf."

"Do you think so?" she cried, raising wide eyes to his face. "I hate to ask, sir, but you must know I am at my wits' end! And I don't dare confide in my uncle."

"Of course not," he soothed, giving her hand a reassuring pat. "Now . . . er . . . where did you say the duke met his superior?"

Jacinda stiffened at the interest in his voice. "Well, naturally I have no way of knowing for certain," she said cautiously. "But I am assuming it was Dover as that is where I am to be taken. And it is where he went yesterday, although I suppose the coach could have stopped somewhere along the way. Perhaps I should ask the coachman . . ."

"I'll see to that," he promised her. "If you ask questions the duke is bound to get suspicious, and that is something you don't want. Did the duke say when you were to be taken to Dover?"

"Some time within the next week." Her lips twisted in a parody of a smile. "I have been given a few days' grace. Isn't that generous of him?"

"Quite generous, and it will give me the time I need to contact Marcus and some other people I know. Never fear, Miss Malvern, I'll see to it that you aren't locked up without any hope of defending yourself against these ludicrous accusations."

"Thank you, Lord Jonathan, there are no words

to express my gratitude. But you won't tell anyone, will you? About my being Lady X, that is,"
she added, ducking her head in a show of maidenly shame. "Things will be difficult enough as it
is without everybody knowing."

"I have given you my word," he replied with a
bow. "Now I think it best that we return to the
house. There is a great deal to be done if we hope
to clear your good name." And he assisted her
onto her horse, the two of them silent as they
rode back to the stables.

Jacinda spent the afternoon helping the servants add the finishing touches to the flowers and
conferring with the cook. Both Lady Shipton and
Cassandra had retired to their rooms to rest for
the evening's festivities, and as usual it fell to her
to handle the myriad small crises that arose. She
was sitting in her study going over the seating
arrangements for dinner one final time when the
door swung open and Anthony strode in, his face
set in a forbidding frown.

"Good afternoon, Your Grace," she greeted him
with a cautious smile, her eyes flickering past him
to the door that still stood open. "Is there something I can do to help you?"

"Blast it, Jacinda!" he snapped, kicking the
door closed with his foot. "What the devil do you
mean by riding out to meet Grayson?"

"I thought that was what I was supposed to
do," she reminded him, her hazel eyes bright
with resentment. "You said—"

"That was before he locked us in the room!"

Anthony interrupted, standing in front of her desk with his arms folded across his chest in a belligerent stance. He had just returned from the stables, and he wasn't in the best of humor. When he learned that Jacinda had returned from her ride accompanied by Grayson he'd known a moment of sheer terror. That terror was quickly replaced by fury that she had gone ahead with the plan without first consulting him, and her mocking defiance did little to soothe his lacerated emotions.

"Didn't it occur to you that as he was responsible for locking us in that he already suspected a connection between us?" he demanded harshly. "You're lucky he didn't throw you off the cliffs and be done with it! I told you, the man is a dangerous and cunning killer!"

"Well, I'm sorry to disappoint you, but he didn't do anything other than offer to intervene with the prince on my behalf," she informed him with a toss of her head. Because she had been doing housework, she had tucked her light brown hair beneath a mobcap and she looked every inch the proper lady—an effect quite spoiled by her defiant glare. "Would you care to hear what he said?"

Anthony hesitated, unwilling to back down and yet needing to know what had transpired. In the end duty overruled his anger, and he settled in one of the Queen Anne chairs facing her desk. "What happened?" he asked, crossing one booted foot across the other.

Jacinda smugly reported their conversation, delighted at the clever way she had handled herself. But if she expected praise from Anthony, she was sadly disappointed. When she finished talking, he leaned back in his chair, his shuttered expression giving away nothing of his thoughts.

"You said he was walking up from the beach?" he said slowly, his mind sifting through all the information she had given him. "Did you see anyone else about? Or a ship off in the distance, perhaps?"

"No," she answered slowly. "There were just the two of us, and there certainly wouldn't be a ship anchored offshore after last night's storm! They would have all put out to sea to ride it out."

"What's down there?"

"I don't know . . . nothing really, just a few caves. But he wouldn't have gone in there."

"Why?" He sank lower in the chair, resting his chin on his hand as he studied her.

"Well, they'd be flooded, of course," she answered, frowning at him. "Besides, even when the tide is low it's dangerous to go there. The smugglers use them to store their brandy . . . especially when the excise men are about."

"Are these caves easily accessible from the cliffs?"

"If you know where to look, but as I said, it's dangerous especially after a storm like last night. The ground above them is weakened, and there have been cave-ins in the past. I'm certain he wouldn't have gone inside one of them."

"Perhaps not, but it still bears investigation," he decided. "Perhaps he's arranged to meet some of the smugglers there so he can pass his information directly to France. Or he could be looking for a hiding place."

"That's a possibility," Jacinda conceded, remembering the one time she had dared explore the caves. "Some of them are quite large, and it would be easy for a man to hide in them and never be seen from the cliffs. There are the smugglers, of course, but if they knew he was there . . ."

"Then they would doubtless assist him." Anthony rose to his feet, his pulses racing with anticipation. "I believe I'll go out now and have a look at them. In the meanwhile, I want your word that you'll stay away from Grayson. From what you've told me he's likely on his way to Dover, but should he still be about, keep well away from him. Understood?"

"Understood." She rose to her feet and walked around the desk to stand before him. "But shouldn't you warn Sir?" she asked, her hazel eyes searching his. "He is in danger. . . ."

"Sir can take care of himself," he assured her softly, reaching out a hand to stroke the gentle curve of her cheek. "As can I, Jacinda."

She trembled beneath his touch, her pulses racing at the feel of his warm flesh caressing her own. Unable to resist his nearness, she covered his hand with her own, pressing it against her lips. "Be careful, Anthony," she pleaded, placing a soft kiss in the center of his palm. "Please be careful. If anything were to happen to you . . ." Her voice broke, and she was unable to continue.

Anthony's heart thundered at the innocent touch of her lips. Her eyes were deep, iridescent pools of green and gold, and he felt as if he were drowning as he gazed into them. His other hand came up to cup her chin, and he rubbed the pad of his thumb across her mouth, sensitizing the warm flesh moments before his lips claimed hers in a kiss of passion and promise.

Jacinda's eyes closed at the feel of his mouth moving urgently against her own. Of their own volition her arms crept about his neck, pulling him close as her lips parted shyly to accept his tongue. The intimate caress made her gasp with pleasure, flames of desire consuming her as she melted into his arms.

"Jacinda," Anthony groaned, his voice made husky with the force of his passion. She was as warm and vital in his arms as he had dreamed she would be, giving herself to him with a sweet gentleness that made him burn with the need to possess all of her. Only the knowledge that this was neither the time nor the place kept him from deepening the embrace. Reluctantly he raised his head, brushing his lips over hers in a final, loving kiss.

"Ah, Jacinda, what have you done to me?" he murmured, his silver eyes lambent as they studied her moist, inviting lips. "You are surely a sorceress to tempt me so."

Her eyes fluttered open at his wry voice, and a soft blush touched her cheeks as she met his gaze. "An . . . Anthony," she stammered, unable to hold back the words that tumbled from her lips. "I love—"

"No." He silenced her by placing his lips over hers in a fleeting kiss. "Not now. Later, when Grayson is safely out of the way. Then we shall talk, I promise you." He gave her a parting kiss, then stepped back. "I'll see you at the ball, my darling," he said softly, turning to open the door. "Mind you save me a dance." And with that he was gone, leaving Jacinda staring after him, hope and love shining in her eyes.

Chapter Twelve

Deciding against taking a mount, Anthony struck out for the caves on foot. He took the precaution of informing his valet of his plans, instructing John to ride to Dover for reinforcements should he fail to return. Not that he expected any trouble—this was only a reconnoitering mission, after all—but Sir had drilled in him the necessity of making contingency plans.

The thought of his superior brought a reluctant smile to Anthony's lips, and he wondered what Jacinda would make of Sir. More than one pretty wench had fallen for the other man's blond good looks and his air of mystery. Not that he wanted her to fall madly in love with Sir, he amended hastily as he scrambled down the rough path, but still it would be interesting.

The first cave he peered into was little more

than a depression in the sheer rock wall, but the second cave had definite possibilities. It wasn't very deep, but it was broad, and could easily hold a man and several barrels of supplies. The third cave was the largest, and his trained eye picked up signs of recent habitation. He rubbed a streak of soot left by a candle, noting that it was remarkably fresh. Smugglers, he wondered, or someone more sinister? The thought made the hair on the back of his neck prickle in alarm, and he withdrew the pistol from his pocket as he approached the back of the cave.

The ground had been swept clean, unusual in a cave, and the depressions left in the wet, hard-packed dirt indicated something heavy had recently been placed there. Not brandy barrels, he decided, tracing the faint grooves with his hand, but something large and square . . . a cache of weapons? He had heard good English rifles had been turning up on the peninsula in the hands of the enemy, but no one could trace the flow. He tucked the information in the back of his head for future reference and moved to the far side of the cave, searching its wet surface for any sign of a crack that would reveal a secret wall.

It was quite dark at the back of the cave, and Anthony wished he had thought to bring a lantern with him when he heard the noise behind him. He swung around, bringing his pistol up defensively, but before he could get a shot off he was struck across the head. Bright colors exploded in a painful blast inside his head, and his last thought as unconsciousness claimed him was of Jacinda and of how much he loved her.

* * *

"Ah, good, Jacinda, there you are," Lady Shipton said, smiling as Jacinda approached her. "It's about time you got here. Where have you been?"

"In the kitchen, Aunt," Jacinda replied, keeping the rancor out of her voice with the greatest difficulty. The ball had been under way for almost two hours now, and this was the first chance she'd had to partake of the festivities. The new gown of rose silk she'd had made up for the evening had become wilted from the heat in the kitchen, and she could feel her hair slipping out of the lover's knot she had spent hours arranging.

"Oh, well, you haven't seen the duke, have you?" Lady Shipton didn't seem to notice her niece's bedraggled condition. "The wretched man has disappeared, and dearest Cassandra is beside herself with mortification. She was counting on his grace to lead her out once the dancing starts."

Jacinda paled at this news. "Anthony is missing?" she gasped, her blood chilling in horror.

"Jacinda! Such cheek!" her aunt declared in an accent of disbelief. "Since when have you been referring to the duke in so familiar a manner? Such forwardness in a female is not to be—"

"When was the last time he was seen?" she interrupted, not caring what she revealed in her agitation. "Did he come back from the cliffs?"

"The cliffs?" Lady Shipton said, blinking in confusion at her niece's tone and the frantic look in her eyes. "How should I know that? The last I heard he was still in the house. But that doesn't answer my question, young lady. I want to know—''

"Has anyone talked to his valet?" Jacinda asked, her eyes going to the gold-leaf clock on the mantel. It was almost nine o'clock, six hours since she'd last spoken to him. If he'd gone to the caves he should have been back hours ago. Unless . . . "What of Lord Jonathan? Is he missing also?"

"Of course not!" Lady Shipton exclaimed indignantly. "He was in the conservatory a few minutes ago. What does one have to do with the other? Really, Jacinda, are you quite sure you are feeling all right? You haven't been yourself at all these past few weeks."

Jacinda didn't bother answering her aunt, and picking up her skirts, she turned and ran from the room, brushing her way past several guests as she ran up the stairs. She found the door to Anthony's room standing open and she rushed in, glancing around her wildly. It was as neat as it had been last night, without so much as a cushion out of place. She stood in the center of the room, chewing on her lips as she realized she had no idea what to look for. She was trying to gather the courage to search his bedchamber when the door opened behind her.

"Anthony!" She whirled around, delight on her face. "Where have you . . . oh." Her voice trailed off at the sight of Peter standing in the doorway, his arms folded across his chest as he surveyed her. "What are you doing here?" she asked in confusion.

"What am I doing here?" His brow raised loftily. "Dear girl, a better question might be, what are *you* doing here? These are a gentleman's private chambers, you know, and hardly the sort of place for an unmarried female to be. Allow me to escort you back down to your aunt and uncle."

"Not now, Mr. Blakely," she replied impatiently, striding determinedly toward the inner door. "This is a matter of the greatest importance, and I can't be bothered with propriety just now."

"Yes, propriety is often a bother," Peter agreed cheerfully, following her into the bedchamber. "And I am always glad to dispense with it." He watched as she searched through Anthony's wardrobe and chest. "I should be more than willing to help you in your search, Miss Malvern, if you would only be so kind as to tell me what it is you are searching for. Billets-doux, perhaps?"

"No!" she said, turning her attention to Anthony's trunk, which she discovered beside the wardrobe. "I don't know what I'm looking for! But there must be something that can help me know what to do."

"About what?"

She glared up at him from her ungainly position hunched over the trunk. He was dressed in an exquisitely cut jacket of bright yellow satin, his cravat tied in an excessive knot. He looked every inch the dandy, but there was something in his blue eyes that made her pause. She studied him in silence before asking quietly, "How much do you know?"

"Enough to know that you could use some help," he replied with a smile. "My good taste and breeding may have been in question from

time to time, but never my intelligence. I take it
his grace is in the employ of the crown?''

At her incredulous stare he shrugged his shoulders. ''You needn't look so surprised, Miss
Malvern. I'm not totally without a modicum of
patriotism, and I know there are many ways to
serve one's king. I've never worked with the duke
before, but I'm not unaware of his . . . shall we
say, interests?''

Jacinda rested on her heels, her mind racing as
she weighed whether or not she should confide in
Peter. But in the end she realized she had no
choice; on her own there was nothing she could
do to help Anthony.

''He went to check the caves,'' she said, struggling to her feet. ''And he hasn't come back.''

''That's what his valet said shortly before he
left for Dover,'' Peter replied, hurrying to help
her up. ''Until he returns I suggest we sit and
wait. There's nothing we can do without—''

''But I don't want to wait!'' she cried, all but
consumed with anxiety. ''Don't you understand?
Anthony could be hurt! He could be d-dying, and
I've got to do something!''

''What?'' Peter asked with maddening practi-
cality. ''We have no idea where he is being held,
or if indeed they are holding him. We don't even
know who 'they' are. No, my dear, I think it best
if we go back to the ball and act as if nothing has
happened. When the troops get here—''

''The caves!'' she interrupted with certainty.
''They are holding him in the caves, I know it!
That is where we must start our search.''

Peter tried reasoning with her. ''But, Miss Malvern, it is dark outside. And in case it missed your notice, there is a storm brewing out there every bit as fierce as the one we had last night. Attempting to climb down the cliffs under such circumstances would be the worst kind of folly."

"I don't care!" she cried passionately, her mind racing ahead to the supplies they would need. "I've got to try, and besides, this could be our only chance!"

"What do you mean?"

"Under the circumstances you have just described, would *you* be expecting a rescue attempt?"

A slow smile spread across Peter's face. "By gad, Miss Malvern, I do believe you are right! I'd be expecting the enemy to hold off until morning, and by that time I would have fortified my position. But an attack in the night, and in the thick of a storm . . . brilliant, my dear, positively brilliant! They won't suspect a thing!"

"We'll need ropes," Jacinda said, pleased with the quickness with which Peter grasped the situation. "And weapons, of course. I don't suppose you have any pistols or such with you, do you?" She eyed him hopefully.

"Just one," he answered with an apologetic shrug. "And I doubt it should do us much good."

"Uncle has some in his gun room. Plus the dueling pistols he keeps in the game room," Jacinda replied quickly. "He keeps the ammunition locked up in the case behind his desk, but I could get the key."

"What about reinforcements?" he asked, studying her thoughtfully. "Even armed as you described, we wouldn't do much good against a horde of smugglers."

"Perhaps not, but it wouldn't take a horde to guard just one man. There shouldn't be more than one or perhaps two guards . . . I hope."

"That's so," he said, rubbing his patrician chin. "And a lookout or two. It could be done, especially if one was determined. I take it you are determined?"

"Quite determined," she answered softly, thinking that she would rather perish attempting to save Anthony than to live without him.

"I thought as much," Peter answered with a sigh. "Marchfield is a lucky man." He pulled his watch from his pocket. "It is a little past nine-thirty now. We shall meet in the game room again in, say . . . half an hour. Oh, and Miss Malvern? Do change your gown. One simply can't rescue one's love in a ball gown and dancing slippers. So déclassé, don't you think?"

Anthony had no idea how long he had been unconscious, but when he finally regained his senses he noted the cave seemed even darker now, and a single candle flickered from a bottle set on a crude table. He concentrated on the weak flame, forcing his muddled thoughts to focus as he evaluated his situation. It wasn't good.

His hands were bound for one thing, and his muscles screamed their protest at the confinement. He was also gagged, although he wondered why his captors had bothered. He doubted anyone would be about to hear him even if he did cry out. The thought of his captors brought his head up, and he glanced cautiously around the cave. He was beginning to think he was alone when he saw a man stirring in the shadows.

"Awake, are ye?" the man grunted, moving forward so Anthony could see him. "Thought ye meant to sleep the night away after that little love tap ol' Rafe gave ye." He hoisted the truncheon in his beefy hands for emphasis.

Anthony glared at him over the strip of fabric gagging him. The man was huge, a good six feet four at least, and he was built like a prizefighter with his bulky shoulders and barrel chest. He was almost prodigiously ugly, with a broken nose and a gap-toothed smile, and when he stepped closer Anthony could catch his unwashed stench.

"Not much to say, have ye?" Old Rafe laughed in malicious delight. "Reckon ye'll be a'sayin' plenty when them frogs get a hold of ye. The gentlemen says as how they'll pay in good guinea gold for the honor o' your company. Mind ye be worth it." He gave Anthony a vicious kick in the ribs before returning to his chair and his bottle of brandy.

Anthony grimaced in pain, breathing in sharply through his nose. He was thankful for the pain though, because it gave him something to concentrate on. He rolled on to his side, testing the knots that bound him. They were well tied, the ropes cutting into his flesh as he attempted to work them loose. He ignored the pain and the slippery feel of blood, determined somehow to win his freedom. One thing he did know, even if he failed in his escape, was that he had to try. There was no way he would risk being interrogated by the enemy. There was always the sea, and if it proved necessary, he knew he would choose a watery grave over betrayal.

"Are you sure about this, Jacinda?" Peter eyed her anxiously from their position crouched behind the rocks. "I still think I should be the one to climb down. I'm the man, after all, and the greatest risk should be mine."

"Yes, and you outweigh me by a good two stone or more," she shot back, securing the thick rope around her waist. "I would never be able to balance you. Besides, I know where the entrance to the cave is located. Don't worry about it, Peter," she added at his continuing silence. "I shall be fine, I promise you."

"You might be fine," he grumbled, taking the other end of the rope and winding it about him. "But I'm not so certain I shall be able to make the same boast once this is all done."

"What do you mean?" Jacinda asked, pulling her riding gloves over her hands. Peter had scoffed when he had seen them, but as she pointed out, they were all she had, as were the neat kid half-boots that covered her feet. She was also wearing her oldest riding habit of black velvet, hoping the darker color would make her less visible when she entered the cave.

"Meaning, my dear, that when Marchfield learns I have allowed you to take this insane risk he shall doubtlessly call me out! And I am hopeless when it comes to duels; couldn't hit a charging elephant with a brace of cannons!"

"That's hardly reassuring at this point," she informed him with a laugh, edging cautiously toward the edge of the cliff. "Although I thought you did an excellent job on those two men we found hiding in the rocks. I daresay they never knew what happened."

"That's true," Peter agreed complacently. "But really, there's no challenge to knocking out a man with a rock, especially when he is already half-unconscious from drink."

"Well, let's hope the men down there are similarly weak-willed when it comes to spirits," she said, staring over the edge of the cliff. Far below her and somewhat to the right she could detect a darker shadow that indicated the opening to the cave. Anthony was down there; she knew it.

"Yes, but if they're not, you do understand what you must do, don't you, Jacinda?" Peter's voice was serious as he cupped her shoulders in his hands, turning her to face him. "You'll have to shoot them; you can't hesitate even for a second because if you do, you'll be dead."

"I know, Peter," she answered softly, her chin coming up as she faced him.

"Killing a man . . . even when there is no other choice, is never easy," he continued in a grave tone, all signs of his usual lightness gone. "You have to live with the memory of his dying expression in your mind, and it's hard, Jacinda; sometimes it's damned hard."

She blinked back tears, reaching up to kiss his cheek. "I know that, Peter, but I can do it. For Anthony, I know I can do it."

He smoothed her hair back with a gentle hand.

"As I said, Marchfield is a very lucky man. Are you ready?"

She grasped the rope about her waist, walking backward to the very edge of the cliff. "Ready."

Anthony bit back a muffled cry of pain as he rolled back onto his side. The ropes were now wet with blood, but he thought they were slightly looser than they had been when he started. That was something, at least. His eyes strayed to his captor, who was propped up against a wall of the cave, his weight sprawled in a crudely made chair that looked unequal to such abuse. Rafe had already consumed a bottle and a half of brandy in the hours since he had regained consciousness, and was well on his way to inebriation. Anthony didn't doubt his ability to get past him, but he had no way of knowing how many men might be posted nearby.

He pushed himself upright, resting his shoulders against the cold surface of the wall. Other than a snort and an incomprehensible mumble, Rafe gave no indication he had heard him, and hope surged in Anthony. Perhaps he would be able to get out of this with his skin still intact, he thought, and in that moment he realized how much he wanted to live.

At first he thought the fall of pebbles was part of a small landslide, like the ones Jacinda had warned him about, and he paid it no mind. But when the sound came again, accompanied this time by a large thump, like the sound of something hitting the front part of the cave, he rose unsteadily to his feet. Rafe jerked at the sound but did not come awake. This might be his only chance, Anthony realized, pushing himself off the ground. If the sounds he was hearing were Rafe's returning companions he would rush past them, and if he was lucky make it outside. If not, there was still the sea . . .

A small shadow crept forward, a slender arm upheld, and in the next minute Rafe was sprawled on the floor of the cave, blood seeping from a gash on his head. The figure stepped across Rafe's prostrate form, and Anthony felt the ground tilting dangerously beneath his feet as the faint light of the candle fell across the features of his rescuer.

"Anthony! Oh, Anthony, my darling, you're alive!" Jacinda rushed forward, her arms going about Anthony, and lowering him carefully to the ground.

"I've been so worried about you!" she scolded through her tears, gently untying the gag. "I knew you were here, but we couldn't figure out a way to reach you, and—"

"What the hell are you doing here!" he rasped the moment the filthy rag had been removed from his mouth. "Get out of here before the others come back and find you!"

"If by the others you mean those two up in the rocks, you needn't worry about them," she said, turning her attention to the ropes about his wrists. The sight of the bloodstained strands and his torn flesh made her bite her lip, but she kept her voice steady as she continued. "Peter knocked them out with a rock and left them tied up for the soldiers to find. They should be here by morning, by the way. Your valet left to fetch them hours ago."

"Hurry up, blast it!" Anthony said, keeping his eyes trained on the cave's opening. He could barely accept the fact that she was here, and yet in a distant part of his mind he wasn't the least bit surprised. Since when had Jacinda ever done what he had expected of her? "Can't you cut those ropes any faster?"

"There's so much blood it's hard to tell where the ropes leave off and where you begin."

"Just hurry," he gritted, wincing as he flexed his fingers. A moment later the tiny knife Jacinda had pulled out of her pocket sliced through the remaining ropes binding him, and he impatiently threw them away.

"Where's Peter?" he asked brusquely, brushing aside her attempts to help him to his feet. He swayed for a brief moment, but after his initial rejection of her aid Jacinda made no move to help him. His curt refusal to accept her help and his harsh manner since the moment she had entered the cave left her feeling hurt and confused. She told herself she hadn't expected cries of undying gratitude, but the least he could do was thank her, she thought, anger chasing out her pain.

Anthony bent over Rafe's inert form, removing a wicked-looking pistol from the unconscious man's pocket and shoving it casually in the waistband of his trousers. "Where's Peter?" he repeated, scooping up the knife and the other pistol Rafe had taken from him earlier. "I assume he's somewhere about?"

"He's up there." Jacinda pointed at the opening

to the cave. "He held on to the rope while I climbed down, and—"

"He let you climb down?" Anthony interrupted, his brows lowering in a dark scowl. "The damned fool! What if my guard hadn't been overtaken with liquor? Do you have any idea what might have happened to you?"

She tilted back her head to meet his icy stare. "Oh, yes," she said in a dulcet tone. "Peter was quite graphic on that point, but I came anyway. Now if you're quite done scolding me, do you think we can be on our way? I believe you said it was dangerous for us to remain here?"

Anthony shot her a fierce look, then swung on his heel and led her out onto the narrow ledge that served as the cave's opening. Another battle erupted as to who would ascend first, and in the interest of harmony Jacinda went first, deciding it wasn't worth the battle. A second later, Anthony stood beside them.

"Where's Grayson?" he asked, once he had untied the rope from about his waist.

"Indulging in some of the earl's finest sherry last I saw of him," Peter replied, fastidiously wiping his hands on the handkerchief he pulled from his pocket. "That snake Aimsford was with him, so we can assume he is a part of this as well."

"You know about Aimsford?" Anthony studied Peter sharply as they began the journey back to the Hall.

"Oh, yes, the scope of my knowledge is indeed surprising," Peter drawled with one of his smug smiles. "It will be a pleasure to bag them both. I've had my eye on the dear marquess for some time now, and I rather fancy the notion of seeing him carted off in chains."

Anthony digested this in silence. He knew Sir's was not the only organization operating in the highest level of the ton, but it did surprise him that the sardonic little dandy was a member of such a group. "What about the others?" he asked, treating Peter with the same respect he reserved for Sir. "How involved are they?"

"Innocent as a batch of lambs, the lot of them," Peter assured him. "Our friends may expect no support from that quarter, I promise you. I assume you intend to take them tonight?"

"I have no choice," Anthony replied grimly, disliking the notion that his carefully laid plans had fallen through. "I have no way of knowing when Sir . . . when my superior will arrive with his forces, but I can't risk having Grayson escape in the meanwhile. Let's hope he hasn't already slipped away."

"Oh, I shouldn't think so." Peter helped Jacinda over a particularly rough stretch of ground. "And in any case, where would he go? The rain has stopped, thankfully, but the sea is still dangerously high; even the most intrepid of sailors wouldn't attempt a landing in such weather. And the roads are being watched by . . . associates of mine, so he wouldn't get very far. I'm sure he will be sitting as tight as a nabob in his harem. I can't wait to see the expression on his face when you walk into the room," he added with a satisfied sigh. "It will even be worth sacrificing my best jacket to witness it."

Jacinda listened to the spy talk flowing about

her, growing increasingly resentful with each step she took. The pair of them sounded like a couple of schoolboys discussing routing their enemies, she thought, stumbling over a tree root. They seemed to thrive on the danger, the excitement, and she wanted to shake them until their teeth rattled. Especially Anthony, she decided, her gaze sliding to her beloved's profile.

What on earth ailed him? Outside of berating her in the cave and on the ledge, he hadn't said above two words to her. After that tender kiss in the library she had thought . . . had hoped he returned her affection, but apparently she had been deluding herself.

Thank heavens he had stopped her from blurting out her love, she decided gratefully. It would have been too humiliating if he knew the true depths of her feelings for him. Unless . . . she stumbled again as the sudden thought occurred to her . . . unless he already knew. Was that why he had stopped her? Why he was treating her so cavalierly now? Was he trying to discourage her, to let her know her affections weren't returned?

"Can't you watch where you're going?" Anthony jerked her up as she was about to fall. "And hurry, I'd like to catch my suspect before he expires of old age!"

The ball was still underway when they crept in through the back. The maids and footmen took time out from their many chores to gape at them, going back to work only when the cook threatened to douse them with boiling water. Anthony's valet hadn't returned yet, and so he sub-

mitted to the butler's ministrations, his silver
eyes resting on Jacinda as she turned to leave the
room.

"I want you to change and go back to the ball,"
he instructed, trying not to flinch as the butler
tended his wounds. "And for God's sake, stay
away from Grayson! The man is probably armed,
and he's bound to be desperate."

"Yes, Your Grace. As you say, Your Grace. Will
that be all, Your Grace?" Jacinda retorted, dropping into a low curtsy that looked decidedly odd
in her bedraggled state. Her eyes were glittering
with challenge when she raised her head to meet
Anthony's narrowed gaze.

"For the moment," he replied, his lips twitch-
ing as he fought the urge to laugh at her fury.
"But you may rest assured I will be having a private word with you once this has been resolved."

Her loud sniff was eloquent as she turned and
stalked majestically from the kitchen, her dirt-
smeared nose held high in the air.

Chapter Thirteen

It was approaching midnight when Jacinda
slipped quietly into the ballroom. With her
maid's scolding assistance she had changed back
into her rose ball gown, her hair pinned in a simple chignon. She hoped no one would notice the

change. Then she ruefully shook her head. When had anyone ever noticed her appearance?

The first person she saw upon entering the crowded room was Lord Jonathan, who was dancing past her with a pretty blonde held in his arms. At least he was still here, she brooded, taking a restorative sip of the icy champagne she had procured from a hovering footman. Heaven only knew what Anthony would have done if Grayson had escaped; hauled her off to Newgate, no doubt!

"And where have you been?" Lady Shipton materialized at her side, her plump face rigid with fury. "We have been looking for you for the past two hours! And don't give me that fustian about being in the kitchen," she added when Jacinda opened her mouth in protest, "because *I* looked!"

"I had to go out, Aunt Prudence," Jacinda replied, taking another sip of champagne. Peter had just entered the ballroom and was bowing to her uncle. She didn't see Anthony yet, and wondered if he meant to stay in hiding until it was time to spring the trap.

"Go out? Go out where?" her aunt demanded, obviously not satisfied with her explanation. "What sort of answer is that? Where did you go, and who did you go with? Really, Jacinda, you can be so thoughtless at times! Didn't it occur to you that your uncle and I might have need of you here?"

The charge of thoughtless on top of all she had endured that evening brought Jacinda's temper flaring to life, and she rounded on her aunt with a militant gleam in her eye. "I was climbing down the cliff on a rope so that I could rescue the duke, who was being held prisoner in a smugglers' cave!" she snapped, her jaw coming forward pugnaciously. "Does that answer your question, ma'am? Or shall I tell you about the three men we left tied up as well?"

Lady Shipton drew herself erect, her double chin quivering with anger. "Very well, Jacinda," she said in an arctic accent. "If you don't wish to tell me the truth, then so be it. But if you think I intend to let this pass, then you are sadly mistaken. Tomorrow morning, missy, you, your uncle, and I shall be having a little chat. You may depend upon it." She nodded once, the purple plume in her turban bobbing stiffly as she turned and stalked away.

Jacinda watched her go, still angry but regretting her flash of temper. Now on top of everything else, she would have to come up with some plausible story to please her querulous relations, as well as acting the role of the apologetic niece. It was not a pleasant prospect, and the very thought of it made her signal the footman for a second glass of champagne.

"Dutch courage, Miss Malvern?" Peter asked, pausing before her, his lips tilted in a teasing smile. "For shame. I thought you were made of sterner stuff than that. Any female who willingly faces armed smugglers shouldn't fear anything."

"Armed smugglers are babes in arms compared to my aunt," she grumbled, lifting the glass to her lips. "Now I shall have to apologize to her on the morrow, and I'm not all that sure I can do it."

"Nonsense, ma'am," he said briskly. "As I have

observed, you can do anything. Now, enough of your tiresome aunt. You've seen our boy, I presume?"

"Indeed." Jacinda was grateful for the change of topic. "Watching him, one would think he hadn't a care in the world."

"Mmm. A prerequisite for being a spy is that one must be a consummate actor, deception being of the utmost importance. But he is more nervous than you might think. Watch his eyes. See how they are always moving? He is obviously expecting someone . . . or something."

Jacinda did as she was instructed, noting that though Lord Jonathan's charming smile never wavered, his eyes kept drifting toward the door. Suddenly he turned his head, his dark eyes meeting hers before he glanced away.

"Do you think he suspects anything?" she asked Peter anxiously.

"There's only one way of telling, isn't there?" he replied, turning to her and dropping a formal bow. "Miss Malvern, may I have the honor of this dance?"

"Why, yes, you may, Mr. Blakely," she answered, her eyes beginning to sparkle in anticipation.

A set for a new dance was forming as he led her onto the floor, and she noted Lord Jonathan was now partnering a sloe-eyed brunette whom she recognized as the older daughter of one of the neighboring squires. The girl's gown of cream silk sprinkled with brilliants provided an excellent foil for Jonathan's dark looks and elegant jacket of midnight-blue satin, and she felt it would be relatively simple to keep her eye on them.

"Ah, I can see our good friend has excellent taste in partners," Peter remarked, taking Jacinda's hand in his as the musicians struck up a tune. "Good, I was terrified I should be forced to dance with some aged dowager."

"What do you mean?" Jacinda asked, following his lead while keeping Jonathan in sight. "You are dancing with me."

"For now, but when the time comes to change partners I shall have the lovely Miss Wallingford, while you get the handsome Lord Jonathan. Rather neat, eh?" He glanced down at her for approval.

Jacinda missed a step. "But Anthony told me I wasn't to dance with Jonathan," she protested, remembering the crystal glitter in his eyes as he issued the command. "In fact, he strictly forbade it!"

"Oh, come, Jacinda, don't be such a milk-and-water miss!" Peter reproved her with a sulky pout. "Since when do you follow the good duke's orders? Besides, what possible harm could befall you in a crowded ballroom?"

That was so, Jacinda thought, moving about the dance floor in time to the stately music. And as Peter said, she was under no obligations to follow Anthony's orders. The memory of those orders as well as the others he had barked at her on the return trip to the Hall was all it took to decide the matter in her mind. She was an independent female, and it was time Anthony realized that fact.

"What do you want me to do?" she asked as Peter adroitly maneuvered them closer to Jonathan and Miss Wallingford. The music was changing tempo, and soon it would be time for the dancers to change partners.

"Smile, flirt, and say absolutely nothing," he advised. "If he asks you anything at all about either Marchfield or me, put him off with some pretty story. And no matter what, don't allow him to talk you into leaving the company. All right? Now!" And he whirled away in a half circle, leaving Jacinda to move on to her new partner.

"Good evening, Miss Malvern," Lord Jonathan said, his hand capturing hers as he led her about the floor. "How fortunate to see you have recovered from your malady."

"My malady, sir?" she inquired brightly, trying not to jerk away at the feel of his cool hand holding hers. "I'm afraid I don't know what you mean."

"Why, the mysterious ailment that kept you absent from the ball for well over two hours, of course," he replied, his brown eyes staring down into hers. "Your aunt put it about that you were suffering from some unfortunate ailment or another. I'm happy to see it was nothing serious."

"Oh, no, a headache, nothing more," she said with a forced laugh. Anthony had just entered the room, accompanied by a tall blond man, and at the sight of her in Jonathan's arms he came to an abrupt halt.

"Ah, yes, that most convenient of feminine complaints," he agreed with a sugary smile, his hand tightening on hers hard enough to cause pain. "Miss Malvern, it might interest you to know that I have a loaded pistol in my pocket, and if you don't come with me . . . quietly, I might add, I'm afraid I shall be forced to use it."

Jacinda stumbled, her eyes going automatically to Anthony's face.

"No, I shouldn't attempt it if I were you." Jonathan followed the direction of her gaze. "Even if I were to miss you, there's no telling who I might hit. Your aunt, your lovely cousin, your lover." He smiled as she stiffened in alarm. "Yes, I rather thought that would get your attention. Now, I want you to walk out of here with me, and remember, I shall have my pistol aimed at Marchfield the entire time. If anyone attempts to stop me, I shall shoot him."

"You can't hope to get away with this," she said, her limbs quaking with fear for Anthony. "You'd be cut down before you could take two steps!"

"Perhaps," he agreed with an indifferent shrug, slipping his arm about her waist and turning her toward the door. "But then, I have been a dead man since this all started. At least I would die knowing I killed Marchfield. And Sir, if I am lucky. After you, Miss Malvern."

"What in blazes is she doing?" Anthony demanded, his hands balling into fists as he watched Jacinda and Grayson moving about the room. "I told her specifically to stay away from him!"

"That was a mistake," Sir replied, his blue eyes

intent upon the couple. "Don't you know one should never order a woman to do anything? Especially a willful and headstrong young woman like Miss Malvern."

"When all of this is over, I swear I will give her a shaking she'll never forget!" Anthony vowed in a strained voice. He had seen Jacinda stumble as well as the panic in the gaze she had sent him, and his stomach tightened in fear. Something was wrong.

"I think we may have a problem," Sir said, his voice hardening imperceptibly. "Grayson's spotted us."

"What do you think he'll do?" Anthony forced himself to think calmly, knowing if he gave into the panic that was consuming him Jacinda could be hurt.

"We have to assume he's armed, and despite Mr. Blakely's assurances, we have no way of knowing how many accomplices he might have. Aimsford is in the card room, isn't he?"

"Yes, I have one of the footmen watching him. I told him I had noted certain small items disappearing into the marquess's pocket, and you may be sure the man is keeping a sharp eye on him. He won't be able to help Grayson."

"Good. They are coming this way." Sir turned his head, keeping Jacinda and Grayson in his sight. "Judging from the expression on your Miss Malvern's face, I think it likely she has a gun at her back. No, don't do it," he cautioned when Anthony jerked convulsively. "He'll kill her where she stands if we make one wrong move."

"But I have to do something!" Anthony

groaned, agony in his voice as he watched Jacinda and Grayson approaching. "I can't let him take her out of here. You know what he'll do to her once he has made good his escape!"

"I have men all around the house, on the road, and in the woods. He won't get far, I—" Sir broke off abruptly as Grayson paused in front of them.

"Sir, Marchfield, I had a feeling we would be meeting again," Grayson drawled, his eyes going from one face to another. "Although I must admit I didn't expect it would be quite under these circumstances."

"Much to your disappointment, I am sure." Sir's voice was low and deadly as he met Grayson's malevolent gaze. "You're making a grave mistake, Grayson. Give it up so that you might at least die like a gentleman."

"Kicking and gasping out my life at the end of a rope, do you mean?" Grayson smiled coldly, twisting Jacinda's arm, causing her to gasp in pain. "No thank you, my lord. I'd rather take my chances outside."

"Damn your soul, Grayson," Anthony bit out, sweat standing out on his brow as he glared at his enemy. "I'll chase you across the depths of hell if you hurt her!"

"How touching." Grayson's arm pressed Jacinda closer while his hand held her other arm in a painful grip. "It was concern for your safety which made Miss Malvern so eager to do my bidding. Isn't that right, my dear?" He twisted her arm again.

Jacinda bit her lip, but she refused to cry out. She had seen Anthony's expression the first time

Jonathan had hurt her, and she didn't want him
to do something foolish. Her one hope was that
once they were outside she could somehow get
away from Jonathan, giving Anthony and Sir a
chance to shoot him without danger to themselves. It had to work, she told herself desperately, her eyes meeting Anthony's. She had too
much to live for to die now.

"So brave, is she not?" Grayson murmured,
goading Anthony with a cruel smile. "Perhaps
before I kill her I will put that bravery to the
test."

"You won't get far." Anthony forced himself to
speak coolly. "The soldiers won't recognize her
and might think she is accompanying you of her
own free will. Why not take one of us instead?
Why not take me? Imagine how much gold your
French friends would pay to get their hands on
me."

"You tempt me, Marchfield," Grayson said in a
thoughtful voice. "Indeed you do, but I fear I
must refuse. You'd have my throat slit before I
took half a step. No, I think I will keep Miss Malvern instead. She is much more—"

"Jacinda! What do you think you are doing?"
Lady Shipton's sharp voice brought Grayson's
head snapping around, his hold on Jacinda loos-
ening slightly. It was all the opportunity she
needed, as she twisted away, falling to one side as
the roar of gunfire filled her ears.

The next moments were a blur of screams and
shouts as everyone about them scrambled for
safety. Jacinda's nose burned at the smell of gun-
powder, and in the next instant she was being

swept up into a pair of strong arms, rough hands moving over her urgently as if examining her.

"Jacinda, oh, God, Jacinda, are you all right? Were you hit? Did that bastard shoot you?"

Jacinda's eyes flickered open, and she gazed up into Anthony's anxious gray gaze. The rest of the world fell away as they stared at each other, asking and answering a dozen questions with their eyes and their hearts. She raised a trembling hand and brushed the hair back from his forehead.

"I'm fine," she assured him, although her voice trembled slightly. "He didn't hurt me." She tore her eyes from his to glance at the man lying on the floor beside her, blood pumping from the wound. "Is he . . . is he . . . ?"

"Not yet," Sir answered tersely, bending over Grayson and placing his handkerchief over the ugly wound. "He's still conscious, Marchfield. We have to get him out of here before he starts talking. Is there a private place we can carry him, Miss Malvern?" His deep blue eyes sought hers.

"Of course, Sir." With Anthony's help she struggled to her feet. Ignoring her aunt's cries and her uncle's querulous demands to know what was going on, Jacinda stood aside as Anthony and Sir, with help from Peter, picked up Jonathan's bloodstained body. She led them to her uncle's study, watching silently as they laid him down on the morocco leather.

"Shall we send for a doctor, do you think?" she asked Anthony, biting her lip as she heard the stricken man groan in pain.

"It wouldn't do any good," Anthony replied,

his attention on Jonathan. "He's been gut-shot, and there's nothing a doctor can do to help him. He's dying and he knows it. We can only hope he'll cooperate with us before he goes." He spared her a quick glance, giving her a tired smile before adding, "We'll need to question him. Can you see to it we're not disturbed?"

Jacinda took his hint. "Of course," she said gently. "But in the meanwhile, what will I tell the others? They're bound to ask questions."

"Tell them he's an infamous thief wanted by Bow Street," Sir answered, taking a cloth from Peter and attempting to staunch the flow of blood. "That should send most of them scurrying to their rooms to check their belongings."

"Very well, Sir," she agreed, exchanging a final, loving look with Anthony before slipping quietly from the room.

"It's no use, Sir," Jonathan groaned through grayish lips as Sir bent over him again. "Just let me die, damn it."

"I never sit idly by and watch my men die," Sir replied, continuing his efforts. "Even when that man has betrayed me." His blue eyes met Jonathan's gaze. "Why, Grayson? For God's sake, why?"

"Not money." Sweat stood out on Jonathan's face, his lips twisting in pain. "Revenge."

"Against whom?" Anthony asked, moving to stand over the two men. "Sir?"

"This country. This damned country that says the eldest son inherits all while the rest of us are left to get by as best we may," Jonathan said in a low, rasping voice. "For as long as I can remember

I had to stand there and watch while my idiot brother took what should have been mine. You know Marcus, know him for the degenerate he is. But he's the eldest son . . . the duke . . . and there was nothing I could do to stop him while he destroyed our birthright . . . my birthright, too. It should have been mine. I would have made a good duke, Marchfield, you know I would have."

"I know," Anthony answered softly, remembering the younger man's interest in farming and his keen feel for the land and its people. It was a cruel trick of fate that a man with Grayson's abilities should have been left with nothing while a painted dilettante like Marcus inherited all.

"The French have the right of it, you know," Jonathan said weakly, blood coming between his lips as he began coughing. "Power and privilege should belong to those who earn it, not those who inherit it and then suck the life from the land." He began coughing again, and when he finished, his face was as white as the front of his shirt had once been. He closed his eyes wearily.

"Ask your damned questions," he said, his voice scarcely audible. "I'll tell you anything you want to know."

Out in the hallway Jacinda was answering what questions she could. Several soldiers had entered the house and while a stony-faced captain was listening to her uncle's bitter complaints, a sentry took his post in front of the study door. The news that Grayson was a suspected thief met with blanket acceptance, and the guests spent the

rest of the evening agreeing that none of them
had really trusted him.

The shooting and the arrival of the soldiers ef-
fectively ended the evening, and Jacinda wasn't
the least bit surprised when one by one the guests
began drifting away. Her aunt and Cassandra
pounced upon her almost at once, but she put
them off by saying she had taken an oath of secrecy and until she received permission there was
nothing she could tell them. When she saw they
meant to debate the matter, she laid claimed to a
headache and went up to her room, ignoring their
demands that she stay and talk to them.

Despite her concern for Anthony and the hor-
rors she had suffered she fell into a deep sleep,
not awakening until several hours after her usual
rising time. She dressed quickly in a green and
black plaid gown, tying her hair back with a ribbon before rushing downstairs. She found her
family assembled in the breakfast room, but before she could utter a word of greeting her aunt
began speaking.

"So! This is how you pay back our kindness for
taking you into our hearts and our homes!" she
accused, her massive bosom rising and falling in
her agitation. "To think that you could use us so
cruelly . . . so vilely . . . I vow I am sunk with
shame for you!"

"Aunt, what are you talking about?" Jacinda
stared at her in honest bewilderment. "How was I
to know Lord Jonathan was a thief? I was just as
surprised as you when—"

"I wasn't referring to last night's unpleasant-
ness!" Lady Shipton snapped, eyeing Jacinda over

the edge of her handkerchief. "Although I might have known *you* would be in the thick of it! A guest shot down in our own home and soldiers tramping about poking their noses in every pantry and wardrobe . . . the scandal will destroy us all. But then, scandal is something you thrive on, isn't it . . . Lady X?"

Jacinda fell onto her chair with an unladylike plop. "You know?" she wheezed, her eyes going from her aunt's livid face, to the smirk on her cousin's lips, and settling on her uncle's forbidding expression. "But . . . but how?"

"I found this"—he held up the letter she had written to her publisher with his thumb and forefinger—"in my study, and if that wasn't enough to convince me, the duke confirmed your identity. He told us—"

"Anthony told you?" she said, shock spreading through her at her uncle's words.

"He did." The earl's mouth pursed in distaste. "He told me that not only were you responsible for the scandalous things, but that you were even now working on another, and that you had dared include him. He is threatening legal action if they are published. Naturally I have assured him they will be destroyed . . ."

Jacinda shook her head, unable to focus as her uncle's voice droned on. She refused to believe Anthony could be guilty of such cruel betrayal. He had given her his word. And yet, she realized, her heart twisting in pain, what other explanation could there be? The others might know about the first three *Journals,* but only Anthony knew of the fourth, and that she had put him in as a character.

". . . no other choice. Your very presence in this house risks all of our reputations, and I must insist that you leave as soon as it can be arranged," her uncle concluded, regarding her with revulsion. "Naturally, no communication between us will be tolerated. At least, until the scandal dies down. Perhaps in a year or two we might allow you to write us, but actual contact—"

"You needn't worry, Uncle Hugh," Jacinda said, rising majestically to her feet, her eyes shining with unshed tears. "For I wouldn't contact you if I was starving to death in the streets!"

"Well!" Lady Shipton gasped, her mouth dropping in outrage. "This is gratitude, I must say! You're lucky we don't set the dogs on you, you shameless hussy! It's no less than you deserve after the way you've used us!"

"I've used you no less than you've used me," Jacinda snapped, her chin coming up proudly. "For the past four years I have acted as your unpaid companion, housekeeper, and slave, and not once, not once did anyone ever think to thank me! Very well, I will go, and you may be very sure you will never see me again! Good-bye!" She turned to go, almost colliding with Anthony, who had entered the room unseen during the heated exchange.

"Ah, Lady X!" he greeted her, ignoring her family's embarrassed gasp as he pressed a kiss to her cheek. "In fighting form as usual, I see."

"Let go of me, you . . . you traitor!" she gasped, pulling free from his hold and striking him across the face. "I trusted you!" And with that she turned and fled from the room.

Anthony was hot on her heels, catching up with her just as she reached her room. He grabbed the door when she tried closing it in his face, flinging it open as he advanced purposefully toward her.

"Stay away from me, you . . . you spy!" she shouted, angrily swiping at the tears that streamed down her face. "Or are you here to arrest me? Did you lie about that, too?"

"I've never lied to you," Anthony said, then stopped, a slow grin stealing across his face. "At least, not unless it was in the line of duty. And you needn't worry that you'll be arrested. I told you, Sir and I have settled that between us. We decided it would be too awkward if my wife was taken up as a traitor."

"Your wife?" she gasped, glaring at him through incredulous eyes. "You think I would actually marry you after what you've done?"

He shrugged his broad shoulders, enjoying the stormy passion in her hazel eyes. He had doubted Sir's plan at first, but he might have known it would succeed. Sir's plans usually did.

"I don't think you really have much choice, do you?" he asked conversationally. "Once word gets out that you're Lady X, you'll be quite ruined. No other man will want to marry you."

"Then I'll become a governess!" she announced, furious that he would dare offer marriage in so cavalier a manner. He probably expected her to accept, she thought bitterly. He probably thought she would fall down on her knees and thank heaven that he would deign to honor her.

"Do you think so?" He leaned against her wardrobe, tilting his dark head to one side as if considering the matter. "A governess's reputation must be even more impeccable than that of a bride. A gossiping wife might be tolerated by an indulgent husband, but a gossiping governess? No one would dare hire you for fear of what you would write in those delightful *Journals* of yours."

Jacinda paled. Such a possibility had never occurred to her, but now she realized he was right, curse him. No respectable family would have her. "Then I shall live alone!" she announced grandly. "I shall keep writing my *Journals.* And I'll become rich and f-famous, and I shall make sport of all of you!"

"No, you won't." His tone was so smugly superior that Jacinda could have screamed. "You're going to marry me."

"Will I? And pray, sir, why would I want to do that?"

"Probably for the same reason I'm going to marry you," he said, advancing on her until he had her pinned against the wall. "Because I love you, Jacinda." And he swept her into his arms.

At first Jacinda couldn't believe the evidence of her own ears, but as his kiss grew ardent she gave up all thoughts of struggle. She threw her arms about his neck, pressing herself against him as he whispered her love to him.

"I love you, Anthony," she gasped, her lips parting beneath his. "I love you! I love you!"

"And I love you, my dearest Jacinda," he answered, his voice rough with passion as he brushed hungry kisses across her mouth. "Forgive me for betraying your secret, but it was the fastest way we could think of to get you to marry me."

"We?" Her voice caught in her throat as Anthony's hands brushed over her soft curves.

"Mmm. Sir and I, and Blakely too, now that I think of it," he answered distractedly, sliding his mouth down the column of her neck. "We were up half the night plotting our strategy. It was Sir's idea that I tell your uncle you are Lady X." He raised his head, his gray eyes warm with love as they gazed down into her face. "You see, we knew we could depend upon him to toss you out bag and baggage, thus leaving you totally at *my* mercy. Of course, I had a counterplan in place, should you prove recalcitrant . . . as you usually do, my love," he added with another kiss.

"What p-plan?" she stuttered, trying to concentrate on what he was saying.

"I was going to lure you into my room and keep you in there until you were quite compromised," he replied, his devilish grin widening at her rosy blush. "Blakely was all for it, but Sir insisted we try his way first."

"I think I am in agreement with Sir." She caught his hand as it strayed too close to her breast, carrying it to her lips and pressing a tender kiss to his palm. "Are you sure, Anthony?" she asked, her eyes meeting his. "When Uncle puts it out that I am Lady X, there will be the most dreadful scandal. I will be infamous. You can't want a wife who—"

He silenced her with a burning kiss, and it was several moments before either of them could speak. "I would want you even if you were the traitor we first thought Lady X to be," he told her in a husky voice. "I love you, Jacinda, and nothing can stop me from marrying you."

"But the scandal—"

"There won't be any scandal," he replied, smoothing her hair back from her cheeks. "Sir will have taken your uncle aside by now and explained matters to him. By the time he has finished, you may rest assured he won't say a peep to anyone about you or Lady X. And when your aunt learns you are to be the Duchess of Marchfield, she will be all smiles and politeness to you. Especially if she knows what is good for her," he added, his face taking on a hard look that was wonderfully familiar to Jacinda.

She kissed the look from him, then rested her head against Anthony's chest. Only one thing marred her happiness, but she had to know. "Anthony . . . what about Lord Jonathan? Is he—"

"Yes," he interrupted, his hand threading through her soft hair and holding her to him. "But before he died he told us everything we needed to know. I think, in the end, he was finally at peace."

"What about Peter?" she asked, saddened by the unhappy young man who had caused such problems. "Where is he?"

"Halfway to Dover by now, with Lord Aimsford in tow," he replied. "It seems the good marquess was sending information and weapons to France through some of your local gentlemen."

"And Sir? What—"

"Jacinda, please understand that I cannot talk about what I do," he said, his expression serious. "I'll be honest with you when I can, but when I can't, you must understand. No questions. All right?"

"All right," she agreed, love evident in her eyes as she snuggled closer to him. "Now, about this plan of yours to keep me locked in a room until I am hopelessly compromised—do you think you could explain it to me again? I fear I may have rejected it out of hand."

Anthony grinned, rejoicing in the love he had found. "Gladly, my dearest," he said, gathering her in his arms. "And mind you pay close attention. This is just the sort of thing to thrill the heart of Lady X. And we all know what a hussy she can be." He bent his head, taking Jacinda's lips in a kiss that proved Lord Stiffback was not so proper a character as Lady X had first supposed. In fact, she was beginning to think there might be some hope for him after all.

A Message To Our Readers...

As a person who reads books, you have access to countless possibilities for information and delight.

The world at your fingertips.

Millions of kids don't.

They don't because they can't read. Or won't. They've never found out how much fun reading can be. Many young people never open a book outside of school, much less finish one.

Think of what they're missing—all the books you loved as a child, all those you've enjoyed and learned from as an adult.

That's why there's RIF. For twenty years, Reading is Fundamental (RIF) has been helping community organizations help kids discover the fun of reading.

RIF's nationwide program of local projects makes it possible for young people to choose books that become theirs to keep. And, RIF activities motivate kids, so that they *want* to read.

To find out how RIF can help in your community or even in your own home, write to:

RIF
Dept. BK-2
Box 23444
Washington, D.C.
20026

Founded in 1966, RIF is a national nonprofit organization with local projects run by volunteers in every state of the union.

GOLDEN HEART AWARD
from the
Romance Writers of America

Joan Overfield

The Prodigal Spinster

Sara Belding has her life all figured out and that's exactly why she *doesn't* need her pompous older cousin, who wants to see her properly wed! But with the same determination he used to defeat the French, Lord Mallingham sets about the matchmaking as if it were a military campaign he's bound and determined to win—even if he has to marry the girl himself!

ISBN: 0-517-00092-X   Price: $2.50

ON SALE NOW!